MARK ANDREW KELLY

FRONT
ROW SEAT

THIS ISN'T A CRIME NOVEL, IT'S A COP STORY

Published by Mindstir Media, LLC
45 Lafayette Rd | Suite 181| North Hampton, NH 03862 | USA
1.800.767.0531 | www.mindstirmedia.com

MINDSTIR MEDIA

Printed in the United States of America
ISBN-13: 978-1-7358689-0-5

This Book is Dedicated to:

224
The cancer took you too soon. You were on
your way to becoming a great cop.

315
Your and your family's display of courage humbles me.

208
We'll never understand why you left us.

251
End of watch 1/23/1999. Never forget.

Introduction

I T HAD BEEN TEN MONTHS since I'd retired from the East Hartford Police Department when members of my old patrol squad invited me out for drinks, an invitation which I readily accepted. We took over a corner of the sports bar we were in and, after some conversation and a couple of beers, I looked at the guys standing around mc. One had shot and killed a suspect who'd come at him with a knife. A couple of years later, this same detective would elicit an admission of guilt from an asshole who'd murdered one of our officers. Another cop in the room had been shot twice in the legs breaking up a domestic dispute, his K9 partner stabbed during the same incident. Both the officer and K9 had returned to duty. A third man had volunteered to stay late and assist on a burglary stakeout one night and parked his cruiser on a highway overpass to survey the area. While sitting in his car, he was struck by a civilian vehicle and severely injured. He spent a month in an intensive care unit and came about as close to death as possible before he started to recover. His injuries prevented him from regaining all of his sight, and he was unable to return to the job (I highly recommend reading his book, *Officer Down, Man Up*, by Todd Lentocha). These were only stories from three of the eight or nine guys there just from my old squad. Other officers in the bar, though not suffering the physical wounds of police work or the burden of having to take a life, had experiences of their own—some harrowing, some funny, some just plain sad. I felt there was a story in all this about what it's like to be a cop but had no idea how to tell it.

A few months later, I was reading a Tom Clancy novel, and the main characters were getting ready to go on a raid. As I read the story, I reflected on my own past raids—many of them—as well as investigative work, undercover assignments, and street work alongside some excellent police officers. Though the Clancy novel was good and entertaining, it was still fantasy, a novel. I wanted to write a real story, a story where an officer, if asked, "What's it like to be a cop?" can point to this book and simply say, "Read that."

I began thinking maybe *I* could write a story about my experiences and, more importantly, the officers I'd worked with. They are, by and large, a group of men and women who, day in and day out, go to work, strap on a gun belt, body armor, handcuffs, and do the best job they can with citizens who don't really want them there, clueless administrators, and a few colleagues who find more satisfaction messing with their co-workers than going out and doing police work. Then they go home and deal with everything else in life: coaching kids' soccer, helping elderly parents, keeping a marriage together, paying the bills, and maybe going out for a drink with their squad.

This book is about patrol officers, the ones who go out each day with the slight expectation of stepping into tragedy. The shift will have ten mundane calls, and all of a sudden, you're in a foot chase, or facing an angry man with a baseball bat, and you're his next target, or entertaining a ten-year-old who doesn't know his mother died unexpectedly in the next room.

Police work is not an easy job to describe. The three protagonists in *Front Row Seat* reflect three different points in a municipal police officer's career. The very beginning, as a new cop, where every experience is new, and you believe each officer you work with is your friend. The middle, as a seasoned veteran, where a promotion is the way out of reliving the same duties over and over—you still believe that you can make a positive change to your organization, and you realize the truth that not all of your co-workers are your friends. The end of your career where the bits and pieces of each case have accumulated in your head for better or worse and the internal department politics have resulted in the same circus with different clowns running the show.

My detective friends are not off the hook, as I have a second book in the works that will delve into narcotics and homicide investigations.

For all of my former co-workers who get past the first few pages of this book and begin to think, *Hey, he's describing me*, all the characters are combinations of personalities and appearances. Really, think about it: There were more than a couple of chiefs who had drinking problems, more than a few slightly overweight balding cops, more than a few with an attitude, etc. Any names that are real are used with permission. All others are works of my imagination.

Preface

THIS STORY IS BASED ON my experiences as a police officer serving the town of East Hartford, Connecticut, from 1991 to 2012. The experiences you will read in the novel actually happened, just not the way I depict them here. Most street names, times, and individuals involved have been changed not just for legal reasons but also because my memory of certain incidents isn't as sharp as it once was, and in many ways, it's just easier to write a novel and make up your own story as you go, kind of like an arrest warrant (Just kidding!).

To give a little background so the uninitiated can better understand the story: Geographically, East Hartford is approximately three miles by five miles, sits across the Connecticut River from the capital city of Hartford, and has about 51,000 residents. The racial makeup is thirty-eight percent white, twenty-six percent black/African American, twenty-eight percent Hispanic, and six percent Asian. A handful of other races make up the balance.

The town has a strong mayor and town council for government, a full-time fire department providing full EMT services, and a police department. Ambulance services are provided by private companies.

The police department is made up of approximately one hundred and twenty officers. For over thirty years, the number of officers, from the chief on down to the newest recruit, has generally been about the same. This puts us within the top twelve percent in size for US departments.

Dispatcher work is its own specialty. We didn't have officers fill in.

Years before I was hired, the police union negotiated with the town a minimum staffing requirement of at least eight patrol officers on each shift along with two supervisors. The most compelling reason for the minimum staffing requirements was officer safety; the availability of a backup officer to either be assigned to a call, or at least be nearby. I point this out because I have met officers from many other towns and jurisdictions who don't have the luxury of almost always having a backup available. There is a big difference between being alone on a bad call and having a partner with you, and it does affect how you react.

There were six ranks in the department: patrol officer, detective, sergeant, lieutenant, deputy chief, and chief. A patrol officer assigned to the detective bureau was called an investigator and was paid at base detective's pay while assigned to the bureau. Some investigators, when the opportunity arose, would qualify for detective and get promoted. Most would return to patrol after a few years of bureau work.

Training provided by the department was, overall, pretty good. Probably some of the best training we had was Simunitions, put on by our firearms staff. It was basically high-end paintball training, the main difference being we used Simunition handguns that were the same as our real guns, but fired bullets made from colored soap. The instructors would set up several different scenarios in which there may or may not be the need to use your gun. In these scenarios, the instructor, following a script, would play the bad guy, and the officer being trained was graded on his or her reaction. Those soap bullets left a mark (and a welt) where they hit. You learned real quick what cover is and if you can fire and hit another person under pressure—completely different from range shooting/target practice. At the end of the day, you could see who was covered in soap marks (put that person on the outer, *outer* perimeter of a gun call) and who wasn't.

I bring this up because it is important to understand that not all officers are equal in all police-related tasks and, even more important, not all departments are equal in their training or even qualification of a new hire. Some departments still use a basic sixty shot-shot qualifying course once a year as their only firearms training. When I see the news of an officer-related shooting and some of the videos that come out, I wonder what training that officer had or the culture in the department. Is there an unwritten rule in their department, or even their own squad, to not call for backup because it makes them look weak? (It happens.) Are they on their own in a rural area with no backup because the jurisdiction can only afford one or two officers on patrol at one time? Are they under pressure from a supervisor to make an arrest even if they're not comfortable doing so? Every police department has its own personality and traits. Most are good; some are not.

Last, I will touch on leadership. There were a couple of chiefs I worked for who were very good, but others were extremely self-serving. (I'm lumping deputy chiefs and chiefs into one group here.) To become a chief, a candidate had to go through the usual interviews, but the choice was already made before the interviews were conducted. It was pretty much a "good old boys club." It's too bad the promotions worked that way because there were a few outstanding candidates passed over who would have made excellent chiefs.

Many years ago, I was a new sergeant having a candid conversation with a new deputy chief, and he asked what I expected of him. I told him, and he glanced at me and said, "I don't have the balls you're looking for in a leader." As a former Marine, I found that admission shocking, but unfortunately, the lack of balls was not limited to that one deputy chief. Welcome to police work!

If you're a rank-and-file cop right now with a few years on the job, you get the picture, and you might keep reading. If you're a chief, you've probably thrown this book away. If you're a civilian, there's a seat for you in the front row, and the show is about to start.

1

Friday
September 2
0003 hours

NEWLY MINTED POLICE OFFICER DONNA Harris put her cruiser in park, exited the vehicle, and slow-jogged to the front door of the low ranch-style public housing unit. No cars drove by, and no noise came from any of the homes. Here the nighttime darkness sucked the light out of the nearby streetlamp, creating a gloom Donna felt in her stomach. Backup police or medical had not arrived yet.

Donna easily picked out the home she had been dispatched to despite the dreary sameness of the block of identical buildings, wood framed ranches and duplexes crammed together on lots barely big enough to fit two vehicles. The residence she was reluctantly heading to on the first call of her midnight shift was the only one with interior light showing through the front door and kitchen window. This was the first time she was the first to arrive, alone, on a call like this.

Donna's legs felt numb as she reached for the front doorknob, double-checking the house number under the bare bulb next to the door. She simultaneously knocked with the butt end of her flashlight and opened the door, announcing herself in a steady voice that belied her fear, "Police, police officer!"

"We're back here," came a woman's voice from the living

room just beyond the small kitchen Donna had entered. She squeezed past the dinner table and chairs that were too large for the small space of the old kitchen. *Maybe this won't be too bad. Whoever is back there sounds calm.* She stepped into the living room. *Oh, shit.*

2

Monday
May 29, Memorial Day
1530 hours
Three Months Earlier

"P ATROL IS WHERE IT'S AT," said Field Training Officer
Gerald Dennen to his new rookie, Officer Donna
Harris. "It's a front row seat to the greatest show
on earth." Almost on cue, the veteran pulled a U-turn on
Main Street, and their marked unit pulled up to the curb
at a bus stop facing the wrong way. "Did you see what was
going on here?" the FTO asked.

Donna hadn't seen anything unusual and wondered why
Gerald had stopped. Gerald continued his brief lecture.
"This job is about reading people, discerning what's normal
at a given time and place, and what isn't normal. Giving a
guy a blowjob at a bus stop at three-thirty in the afternoon
on Main Street isn't normal. Even in this fucked-up town."

Donna still had no idea what Gerald was talking about,
but she'd learn over the next two hours, which would be
summed up nicely in his report:

"While on routine patrol in a marked unit heading south
in the 700 block of Main Street, I observed three parties
standing at the bus stop. In my initial observation, I could
see that two were males, and one I assumed was a female.
My view of the presumed female was blocked by several
newspaper boxes, but I could see her as she appeared to be

kneeling behind the boxes, her head moving back and forth in front of the crotch of one of the males, later identified as Allen Johnson. During this initial observation, it appeared that Johnson had his eyes closed, his head slightly tilted back, and his mouth agape as if he was silently saying *ahh*. At this same moment, I also observed the second male, later identified as Mark Collins, standing next to Johnson with a smile on his face like a child doing something he knows he shouldn't but is too fun to stop. The third party, whose head and face were in front of Johnson's crotch, was identified as Sonia Fuentes. It did appear to me, a trained observer, that the act of oral copulation was occurring in broad daylight, at a bus stop, at about 1530 hours. I stopped to investigate.

"Upon exiting my cruiser, I began to converse with the above parties. I asked them if they were engaged in oral copulation, though based on what I determined to be limited language comprehension skills on the part of all three parties, I asked in a much simpler language they could understand—I asked if Fuentes was giving Johnson a blowjob. They all denied such an act was occurring, though there was no sign of the indignation that would normally arise after such an allegation. All three parties were run through the National Crime Information Center, and a warrant for Johnson was on file. Johnson was taken to headquarters and booked by Officer Harris without further incident. Collins and Fuentes were sent on their way without further incident."

It only took Gerald about fifteen minutes to write the narrative of the report. He could have done it in less, but he was having fun describing his encounter with Johnson and his friends. *Good times,* Gerald thought as he proofread the report. It took Donna nearly an hour to book and process Johnson, an exercise that also used to take fifteen minutes—ten if the cop was really quick—but now, with computerized booking systems, the computer wouldn't let the booking officer finish unless each screen was completed to the computer's satisfaction.

Donna and Gerald headed up to the watch commander's office to have the report reviewed and signed by the sergeant on the desk, Donna grumbling the whole way about the computerized system. Gerald nodded. "The concept is a good one. Basically, we're booking prisoners online, so, for example, all of Johnson's info, including his fingerprints, will be available to all levels of law enforcement—local, state, and federal—in about fifteen minutes. In theory, any cop in the country can run Johnson's name and get the information you just entered. The problem is that not all computer systems talk the same language, like, how not all jurisdictions call the same crime by the same name. Here in Connecticut, we call a burglary a burglary with different degrees of seriousness. In other states, it might be called breaking and entering. The feds might call it something else. That's why what seems logical to us isn't always logical to the computer, and the computer rejects your entry."

"It's not just that," said Donna. "It's the formatting and navigating through the pages. Totally different than how any website works."

"Oh," said Gerald, "That's just an example of inefficient government bureaucracy in the computer age. Try not to get frustrated. The more you use it, the more you'll understand what to enter on each screen. And once you've been on a while, you'll pick up on shortcuts that make the computer happy. As your FTO, I'm just gonna keep showing you the proper way to do things. Shortcuts will be up to you to figure out later. Now, let's head to Dunkin' Donuts—it's your turn to buy," Gerald said as they walked out to their cruiser.

"Why is it my turn to buy?" asked Donna.

"Because you're not a real cop yet. Once you pass your twelve weeks of field training and can handle calls on your own, then you'll be a real cop, and I'll start buying the coffee once in a while."

Being called *not a real cop* pissed Donna off, but she couldn't argue the point. Two weeks earlier, after finishing her four and a half months at the police academy—where she finished number three in her class of twenty-eight—she arrived at headquarters wearing her class B patrol uniform, complete with shiny badge and nameplate.

***

Donna did not always want to be a cop. She grew up in a blue-collar family, her dad working in the paper mill in Millinocket, Maine, and her mother, a homemaker and occasional substitute teacher at the local grade school. After graduating from the University of Maine with a degree in forest management, Donna discovered how few job opportunities there were in the forest service and how little those paid. Young, full of energy, and with a strong desire to move away from Millinocket, she'd started waiting tables and bartending while living with her parents. It was an easy enough life while she saved money.

While bartending one night, she turned from her cash drawer to face the bar just in time to see a male patron slap a woman across the face. The woman lowered her head, as if trying to hide behind her long hair, but didn't cry. The man called her a stupid bitch and gulped down his beer. Donna stared, not quite sure what she should do, wondering what the relationship was between the two, when another man came up from behind the assailant. This second man had the bearing of a military officer. He tapped the bully on the shoulder. "Hitting a woman. That's assault, you know." When the assailant turned, he found himself facing a gold badge in the left hand of the military-looking guy, who then announced very clearly he was a Maine state trooper.

"I didn't ask what your job was," the assailant spat. The trooper smiled, nodding, as the goon turned and ordered another beer. When Donna stepped back, crossing her arms and shaking her head, the trooper made his move, grabbing and twisting the assailant's arm behind his back and pinning his head to the bar. The man was handcuffed in seconds and led out of the bar. A few minutes later, the trooper came back in and talked to the woman. To Donna, she appeared more upset with the officer than with the guy who hit her. After a short conversation, she left the bar. The trooper then talked to Donna, asking what she had observed. Donna said she had seen the man slap the woman. The trooper took her name and address and told her he might contact her, then left.

The next day, Donna woke thinking about the incident the night before. She had seen bar fights before, most ending in the parking lot with few injuries and no need for the cops to come. But something about the trooper being there last night to stand up for someone who couldn't defend herself struck her.

In high school, she had stood by when other kids bullied a classmate, a girl who was overweight with pimply skin. During one lunch break, boys and girls piled their leftover food on her tray, making pig noises. Every day after that, you could tell when the poor girl was walking down the hall because other students would make the same oinking noise. No other students would walk with her or talk to her. One day the girl left school and never came back. Rumor had it she moved to another town, started using drugs, and died of an overdose before her senior year. Donna felt ashamed of never having helped the girl. Maybe one friend or kind comment could have changed her life. Donna, as an adolescent, didn't feel she was able to step up to bullying, didn't know what to say or do, and feared she would become the bullies' new target.

In college, Donna matured and turned her feelings of shame into acts of kindness. She found herself gravitating toward students with disabilities, becoming a friend to several, and offering to tutor students who needed help with their classwork. Helping people made her feel better but didn't quite make her feel like she was making up for her lack of compassion in high school. The state trooper in the bar, he was defending a person who couldn't defend herself. That clicked with Donna: Defend the defenseless, right the wrongs, bring offenders to *justice*. I will be trained to help people who can't help themselves. I can get satisfaction, fulfillment, out of that, she believed. She spent the remainder of the morning looking up police job qualifications.

Over the next year, she applied to six departments throughout New England. She juggled written tests, agility tests, interviews, and polygraphs for each department with travel and her jobs waitressing and bartending. When a sergeant from North Hayward, Connecticut, called to tell her she'd been accepted, she hesitated. She was high on the hiring list for two other departments in Maine, closer to home, but this was a sure thing. The sergeant on the other end pressed her. He told her it might be over a year before they hired again, and if she didn't accept, she'd be moved to the bottom of the hiring list. Donna bit her lip and said yes. A week later, she was in the police academy.

The Connecticut Police Academy in Meriden, Connecticut, hosted police candidates from numerous towns and, for four and a half months, trained them to be police officers. The candidates lived in one wing of the academy in spartan two-person rooms. Donna's class had twenty-eight candidates from seventeen towns. She was surprised to learn one of her classmates was in his late thirties, and one female candidate would turn twenty-one while in the academy. All had had previous jobs—some as volunteer first responders, some former military, one had been a teacher, a few had been security guards or corrections officers. All had displayed through their actions or words the belief that they, as individual police officers, could make things better for the citizens of the communities they would soon serve.

Donna found the hardest part of the academy was the eight hours of classroom time each day, with a one-hour break for lunch. Those hours would be some of the most boring of her life. The physical training wasn't grueling by any measure, on the mats by 06:00, some calisthenics, and a mile and half run three times a week. Classes on criminal law, motor vehicle regulations, search and seizure, victims' rights, suspects' rights, the difference between mere suspicion and probable cause, the strict rules of domestic violence cases, report writing, and exams filled their days. Instructors constantly reminded the candidates that a false arrest or misapplication of force on a citizen would get them fired, and lawsuits could be brought against them.

Donna had taught herself during her college studies to take at least one positive thing away from a class or instructor, no matter how boring. In the four-plus dull months in the academy, Donna remembered one instructor who brought clarity to the difference between being a police officer and doing any other job—a lesson Donna never forgot.

It was during a defensive tactics training class—self-defense for police officers. The candidates were on the mats in the gym learning about the twenty-one-foot rule, which stated that an assailant with a knife would be able to stab an officer standing twenty-one feet away before the officer could draw and shoot his gun. The candidates were skeptical but remained quiet. The instructor then demonstrated by having one of the candidates hold a stopwatch while a second classmate, a former security guard named Bill, secured a dummy gun in his holster. The instructor told the candidate holding the stopwatch to start timing as soon as the instructor started charging Bill and to stop as soon as the teacher touched Bill. Bill was told to draw and shoot the dummy gun as soon as he perceived a deadly threat.

The instructor measured twenty-one feet from Bill and marked the spot with a piece of duct tape on the floor. The instructor stood on the mark, looking at the ceiling, then the ground. Bill stood still, feet shoulder-width apart, tattooed arms folded across his chest, anticipating. The instructor began to turn as if walking away, then suddenly spun and charged Bill. The stopwatch started. Bill reflexively threw his left arm out while his right hand manipulated the securing straps on his holster. The instructor, still charging, pulled out a knife he'd been palming in his hand. Bill began to backpedal. The instructor closed in and plunged the knife. When the weapon found its mark in Bill's stomach, his gun was barely out of the holster. The stopwatch stopped: One point five seconds.

The knife was made of rubber and barely left a mark on Bill, but the candidate's pride had been hurt. He was young, a former soldier with a combat tour under his belt, and in good physical condition. He should've been able to get the make-believe shot off.

"Next," commanded the instructor, taking the dummy gun away from Bill and handing it to another candidate. Three more took a turn. Each time, the instructor was able to stab the candidate before they could draw and shoot.

Donna was up next. She had studied the instructor and felt she could be the one to beat him. She mentally rehearsed drawing the dummy gun and sidestepping, not backing up—a fatal move in a fight—away from the charging instructor. She took her position, and the teacher stood on the mark. He charged, Donna went for her weapon and took a half step to her right. The instructor slowed. Donna almost had the gun up. He stopped and whipped his arm up with the hand holding the knife. Donna yelled, "Bang!"

She won.

The instructor froze when he heard her say bang. He then slowly held out his hands, palms up. In his right hand was a cell phone, not a knife. "You just shot an innocent person," said the instructor.

"But—" Donna started saying.

The instructor cut her off as he pocketed the cell phone. "But what, that wasn't fair? If you're expecting bad guys and citizens, in general, to treat you fairly on the street, you're in the wrong business."

He turned away and walked back to the mark on the floor.

From there, he addressed the class, "You will never have all the information you need when you go on a call, and the information you have received will probably be inaccurate. All of you assumed this drill was just about surviving and winning a knife attack. It is that and more. Next student up!"

The remaining candidates fared worse than those who started the drill. Defend themselves from the knife, unholster, move, knife or cell phone, shoot, don't shoot. Indecision was paralyzing and would get them killed. Shoot an unarmed person and face the dire consequences. Decide in just one point five seconds.

At the end of the class, the instructor called for a school circle; the candidates formed a seated circle around him. "This is the only job in the world where you as an individual may be required to decide to take a life in one and a half seconds or less. All the training you're receiving on how to handle the mentally ill, using less than lethal force, and reading body language are excellent things you need to know and keep in your mental and physical toolbox when dealing with the public. When time permits, use any or all of those tools. But there very well may be a moment when you only have one and a half seconds to take a life, to save a life. To save yourself. And after you've pulled the trigger, it may not be so clear-cut that you did the right thing, as we demonstrated with the cell phone. The rules on the use of force are clear, but the situations you'll be put in are not. The whole reason we need police officers is that people get themselves into unusual situations, and we are the ones called to those situations to straighten them out."

With that, the class was over, but the training stuck with Donna more than anything else she experienced at the academy.

Donna graduated at the beginning of May. Her parents came down for the ceremony, and she proudly wore her uniform for them for the first time. Her father asked what was next, and she told him she would be reporting to the police department on Monday for two weeks of in-house instruction, then twelve weeks of working the street with field training officers.

After going to dinner with her parents—their treat—Donna went home to her small apartment and looked at herself, in uniform, in the mirror. With no one else around to hear, she said, "This is so cool. I'm a cop with a real job, a real paycheck. A cop. Awesome." She smiled a little longer at her reflection before taking off the uniform.

Her first day out of the academy, she found herself at the police station, recently renamed the public safety complex, standing in a hallway between the watch commander's office and the desk officer's post. A few cops walked by and gave her a nod and maybe a "Hi," but nothing more. It was 0800, and she was waiting for someone to come get her to begin her in-house training. The desk officer, a guy about her dad's age with a bald head and a sizable belly, looked her over, then stared at her boobs. He heaved himself out of his chair, approaching her, eyes still trained on her breasts—specifically, her right one. The old cop tapped her metal nameplate lightly and smiled. "Little lady, the first thing you want to do is get rid of the bar under your name tag that says *serving since 2019*. Every asshole on the street will know you're brand new and have no experience. They'll give you no respect and will walk all over you." Donna managed to mumble a thank you.

Moments later, the training NCO led Donna away to a stairwell.

Two veteran officers who had been in the watch commander's office across the hall, came out to offer their unsolicited opinion of Donna.

"She's kinda cute," said one.

"Yeah, just wait until she gets cruiser ass. . . . She's halfway there already," said the second cop.

"It's the uniform pants. No one's ass looks good in uniform pants."

"Mine does," said Sergeant Mitch Reilly as he rounded the corner of the hall and picked up on the last portion of the conversation. "Ask any of the ladies in dispatch."

"I'm not sure I would take an opinion about my ass from one of them as a compliment—they're all nuts in there," the first cop commented.

Reilly didn't break stride as he stepped past the officers and headed to the nearby fax machine. "At least I'm appreciated for something around here."

"You here on overtime again, Reilly?"

"Yes, I am. Just over one hundred days of employment are left in my wonderful law enforcement career. And as we all know, more overtime for me equals a fatter pension for me."

The desk officer, still two years away from retirement, tried not to show any envy. "How long do you think it'll be before one of the young dogs around here tries to get into her pants?" he asked as he settled back into the worn chair at the front desk.

"I bet a few have already tried," Reilly said as he walked across the hall with a fist full of papers to the watch commander's office.

That was the start of the first day of two weeks of in-house training for Donna. Now she was paired up with Gerald on her first day in the field. A little under twelve weeks to go before she would be considered a *real cop*.

3

Wednesday
May 30
2117 hours

"YOU KNOW WHERE WE ARE?" asked Gerald as he placed the cruiser in park.

"Ummm . . . not exactly," replied Donna as she craned her neck around to try to spot a house number or street sign. Her hopes of finding either in the reflections of flashing strobes emitted by their emergency lights quickly faded. She wasn't even sure what street they were on. Instead, she had been focused on observing Gerald as he checked the registration plate, running a listing as he called it, on the vehicle in front of them.

"If you had to call for help right now, what would you tell dispatch? They're going to ask for your location."

"I don't know," Donna said, feeling foolish that she had not paid attention to where they were.

In front of them, stopped next to the curb, was a white Hyundai. Gerald poked at a couple of switches on their console as his eyes stayed focused on the occupants of the parked vehicle. As he did, he explained to Donna, "The white lights on the light bar on the roof are called take-down lights. They will give you more illumination to the front. You also have alley lights that will light up anything to either side. Now, do you see a house number?"

"Yup, fifty-four."

"And what street are we on?"

"I didn't see the street sign."

"We're on Parker Road." Gerald aimed their cruiser spotlight at the registration plate of the Hyundai and said, "See how it's slightly crooked? It's only held on to the bumper by one screw. Odds are that the plate doesn't belong to this car or the car may be stolen or, maybe, the operator has a reasonable excuse." Donna nodded in understanding. Gerald adjusted the spotlight. "Keep as much light as possible pouring into any vehicle you stop. Makes it harder for the occupants to see you approach."

"Uh-huh."

Gerald's fingers clicked the keys on their MDT, the mobile data terminal in-car computer. Seconds later, a message appeared, and Gerald read part of it aloud. "The plate belongs to a red Toyota minivan registered out of Vernon." Looking back up at the Hyundai, Gerald said, "It's hard to tell with the window tints how many people are in it, so we'll assume there's more than just the operator until we know better." Gerald radioed dispatch to advise them of their location and reason for the stop, then climbed out of their cruiser and slowly approached the Hyundai.

Donna mirrored Gerald's movements on the opposite side of the car, dividing her attention between Gerald's half of the conversation and watching the interior of the Hyundai. After a minute, Gerald backed away from the driver's door and motioned with his hand for Donna to stay where she was. Donna focused on the two occupants of the vehicle. In her flashlight beam, she could see the lap of the driver, a woman wearing medical scrubs, sitting very still, clutching an envelope full of forms. In the back seat was a child, maybe three years old, sleeping in a car seat.

After a couple of minutes, Gerald walked back up to the driver's side and leaned into the window. Donna could hear Gerald state that he would give her a couple of business days to make things right and to have a good night. He turned and walked back to their cruiser, waving Donna to do the same.

As soon as their doors were closed, Gerald engaged the transmission and pulled away, at the same time clearing the car stop over the radio with dispatch and clicking off the emergency lights. After they had driven a couple of blocks, Gerald asked, "What would you have done if you had pulled her over?"

"From what I could tell, the vehicle wasn't registered and maybe not insured. I probably would have given her a ticket and towed the vehicle," Donna answered.

Gerald said, "The first part of your answer is correct. The car isn't registered and, therefore, not insured because insurance companies don't pay out on unregistered vehicles."

Donna waited a moment, unsure of how to challenge her FTO, and finally said, "I didn't see you write her a ticket."

"You're right. Do you know why?"

"No."

"Her story is that she just bought the car and to save time and not have to take a day off from work to go to DMV and get a temporary registration, she just slapped a plate on her car that the seller had leftover from another car he used to own."

"So, she *is* driving an unregistered car, and she *is* misusing a plate. Isn't that a slam dunk?" Donna asked.

"Yeah, it's a slam dunk, but she *is* going to insure the car, and she *is* going to properly register it, even though she's barely got a pot to piss in."

"How can you tell?"

"She had the insurance paperwork filled out along with a check to send in inside that envelope she was holding. She has just graduated from school to be a dental technician. She has her kid in a child seat, and she has a prepaid cell phone in the cupholder. From what I can tell, she doesn't have a lot of money, but her priorities are right. You know what I mean?"

Donna remained quiet as Gerald stated his case. "She has a cheap phone but a good child seat. Insurance check is filled out and ready to mail. In my judgment, she's trying to do things right but has to cut a few corners here and there to make ends meet. Trust me, if she had a five-hundred-dollar smartphone and the kid wasn't in a child seat, she would have had a ticket, and the car would have been towed. You get what I'm saying?

"I think so."

"Let me put it another way: Do you think saddling her with a ticket and having her pay a tow charge is really doing her or anyone else any good? Make a note in your notebook to remind us to check on her in one week to make sure she did what she's supposed to do." Donna pulled her new notebook out from her breast pocket, clicked her pen, and copied down the woman's information off the MDT. They were the first notes of her career.

———————

Donna would soon learn that one of Gerald's pet phrases was "good times." He often used it when a situation wasn't necessarily all that good but, in an odd way, funny. Their next call, a half-hour later, was qualified by the dispatcher as a mother-daughter domestic. The dispatcher stated both parties would be out in the driveway waiting for their arrival. Two minutes later, as Gerald guided the cruiser up the street, the headlights illumined two women standing at the end of a short driveway. Donna could hear their voices from three car lengths away with the windows rolled up. The words "bitch" and "fucking bitch" were spread evenly through their argument. Just as Gerald and Donna exited their cruiser, one of the women, later determined to be the mother of the other, backhanded the younger one in the mouth and yelled, "I should have sucked your daddy's dick instead of having you!"

25

"Good times," Gerald said, barely loud enough for Donna to hear.

Gerald and Donna quickly had the two women separated by a few feet, facing away from each other as they listened to their explanations for the confrontation. Gerald, being responsible for handling the case while Donna observed, listened to both women individually, then sent the daughter into the home and addressed the mother.

"Ma'am, you and your daughter are both telling me the same story, which is this: Your daughter, being eighteen, wants to stay out late and be with her friends and you, being a good parent, want her to follow your rules as this is your house." The woman, arms folded high across her chest, nodded affirmatively. Gerald continued, "As a single parent myself, I can totally understand your feelings. I also have a twelve-year-old daughter who thinks she's twenty-two."

"I'm right then," the woman said, the tight grip she had on herself loosening.

"Well, not exactly," Gerald said. "If this was just a verbal argument, a parent correcting a child's behavior, then we would leave now. Unfortunately for you, we saw you strike your daughter in the face with your hand, and that falls under our domestic violence laws, meaning I have to write you a summons to go to court first thing tomorrow morning."

"But I have to work in the morning," the woman protested.

Gerald held up his hands and said, "I'm on your side on this one, lady, but I have to write you the summons. I have no choice in the matter. Take a deep breath, and I'll be back in a minute."

The woman was chatting with Donna when Gerald walked back up to her after filling out the summons. "Here's your summons and instructions on where to go and what to do in the morning." As the mother stared at the summons in her hand, Gerald followed up, "I think you're a good parent, and I don't expect to be called back here tonight." Gerald then flipped his metal clipboard around and finger-tapped the bottom of an attached form. "Your signature here means you promise to appear in court tomorrow morning. If you don't sign, then I have to bring you in to make sure you appear." The woman signed the summons and slowly walked back to her front door, shaking her head repeatedly, muttering how shit ain't right. Gerald and Donna were soon pulling away.

"I didn't know you had any kids," Donna said.

"I don't," Gerald said. "I wanted that woman to relate to me. Did you notice once I told her I have a problem daughter she relaxed a bit?"

"Uh-huh."

"That's one way to de-escalate a fight, get the parties to identify with you. In this case, once she saw me as a single parent, she relaxed a bit." They drove in silence for a few moments then Gerald said, "The first thing anyone sees when you get out of your cruiser is a uniform, a cop, coming to be an enforcer. Sometimes it's good to have them see you as a person first. Other times you have to be the enforcer first, person second."

"I think I see what you're saying."

Gerald then mimicked what he had heard the mother say as they pulled up, *"I should have sucked your daddy's dick instead of having you."*

"That's priceless . . . good times."

4

Saturday
June 3
1730 hours

GERALD AND DONNA WERE OUT on patrol in their cruiser in District Twenty-Five. As Donna drove, she sheepishly asked Gerald, "Do we always have to radio dispatch every time we need to use the bathroom?"

Gerald suppressed a smile and said, "I think I know what you're getting at. Whereas a guy on patrol can pretty much go anywhere to relieve himself most of the time and do it quickly, you ladies need to take a longer respite to find a secure bathroom, such as a firehouse or headquarters."

"Yes," Donna said, "because we are disarming ourselves whenever we take off our gun belts. So I can't use a public bathroom like you guys can, and I take longer putting all my gear back on." Gerald nodded as Donna continued, "I'm getting self-conscious calling off at headquarters four or five times a shift just to use the bathroom."

Gerald nodded. *This wasn't covered in the FTO handbook.* He smiled and said, "Either learn to piss standing up without making a mess or keep calling off when you need a relief."

Donna's expression remained neutral, and Gerald wondered how his flippant reply was being received. After what seemed like a long silence, he said, "We have some old-timers here who take a long time to do anything, including going to the bathroom, and no one complains or takes much notice. If it appears you are using bathroom breaks to avoid calls, you will be singled out by a supervisor or squadmate. But as long as you're handling your calls in a timely manner, no one will give it much thought."

It wasn't the answer she wanted to hear, but she let the topic drop.

Gerald wanted to change the subject and get back to patrol work. He said, "The only way you're going to learn these streets is to drive them. I'll call out a road, and you find it. You can look at your map—in fact, I want you to—until you know this town by heart. The most anxious time you'll have is trying to recall a street or address on a hot call. And even though the cruisers have GPS on the MDT, it's still up to you to get to the address, even if the MDT isn't working or the GPS goes down—which happened to me one time, the whole screen went black while responding to a gun call."

Gerald was still biased when it came to technology. "A good street cop knows his town and doesn't depend on a computer to tell him where to go or what to do," was a phrase he often repeated to the recruits he field-trained over the years.

Gerald Dennen had been a cop for over twelve years. When he was twenty-three, he received his degree in criminal justice and toyed with the idea of going on to get a law degree. Short on cash and long on student loans, he started taking construction jobs and never went back to school.

One sweltering summer afternoon he was laboring over a trench in the street his construction crew was digging for the utility company Connecticut Illuminating. He had taken a break from working the jackhammer and was in the process of picking the tool back up when he heard sirens. With his protective earpieces, he could not at first determine where the sirens were coming from and didn't know they were closer than he thought. The simultaneous sound of screeching tires and crunching metal snapped his gaze to his right, across the street. There he saw a compact red car wedged under the back of a jacked-up pickup truck. The hood to the compact car was bent up, and steam hissed from the broken radiator. Gerald watched as the operator of the red car tried to force his door open but couldn't. Squeezing through the car window headfirst, he escaped from the wrecked car and fell on his back, rolled over, and sprinted across the street. The moment the driver fled his crashed car, a police cruiser skidded to a stop behind it, its driver's door springing open before it had come to a complete stop and the cop running after the fleeing operator.

The driver dashed less than ten feet past Gerald followed by the cop and a German shepherd. More police cars arrived, and cops jumped out with guns drawn. Gerald stepped closer to the large rear wheel of a backhoe and watched. A second person in the compact car had his hands sticking out a window as the cops yelled at him. From behind him, Gerald heard someone shouting "Get him" several times, followed by wails of pain. Moments later, the cop with the dog was escorting the teenage driver, now in handcuffs, grimacing and limping, back to the crash scene.

Gerald felt a rush of adrenaline being this close to police action and took a bit of pride in being able to tell a sergeant later, who informed Gerald that the red car was stolen, what he had witnessed. *That's a job, a career*, thought Gerald. *I could be one of those cops that criminals truly fear.* The next day he began looking into getting hired by a police department.

Hired as a police officer shortly after his twenty-eighth birthday, he had stayed in patrol, working mostly the evening shift. As a new officer, he went all in for the lifestyle of hard work and harder play. While on duty, car chases, foot chases, bar fights, and active robberies were the calls he loved to jump into. When off duty, partying hard, riding his Harley with other cops, and retelling stories of dangerous calls replaced the thrill of the real thing. Outings with non-cop friends became fewer and fewer. They were just too boring.

He dated but never married. He would find a woman he liked, maybe even loved, and be with her for two to three years. Eventually, he would find a new girlfriend and break off the old relationship. Those who knew him long enough knew an expiration date came with each new girlfriend, no matter how pretty or smart. His current one, a blonde lawyer, was in his home now, warming up for a five-mile run.

He had tried working in the detective bureau as an investigator for a while but found it tedious, and after only six months, asked to be moved back to patrol. An average marksman when he got hired, he volunteered to become a firearms instructor and became an excellent shot. One of the biggest challenges he and the other firearms instructors faced was training everyone in the department twice a year. He could tell some officers just didn't have the fight in them if facing a deadly force situation. Those officers would do just enough to get through the training courses, in the back of their minds clinging to the thought that statistically, they would never have to use their gun. Others were enthusiastic but just terrible shots. Most officers appreciated the training and, while instructing a class, Gerald often wanted to say, "There's got to be a part of you that will kill, almost *wants* to, because there are some very bad people out there, and killing them is okay," but he could never say that out loud to a group of police officers. It was way past what was acceptable in today's politically correct climate.

———————•••———————

Donna turned the cruiser onto Burnside Avenue and headed east toward the Village. The Village was a neighborhood built during the '40s to house the many people who worked in the town's factories. It consisted of duplex and ranch homes, connected end to end, with two to four units to a building.

Each had its own entryway; some had driveways. Over the years, factory jobs dwindled, and the demographics of the village had gone from mostly lower working-class whites to a mix of single-parent whites, blacks, and Hispanics. The Asian and Middle Eastern immigrants shunned the Village, and for some reason, the upper Village had more problems that the lower Village, even though both sections had the same racial makeup and building styles. Maybe it was because in the upper Village, more were on government assistance of some kind and didn't have to work—or if they did, it wasn't at a job requiring a lot of cerebral activity or time. Domestic violence, drug dealing, and theft were common.

"Unit Twenty-Five, take an active domestic at forty-two Lockwood Circle. Caller states male and female actively fighting on the front lawn. No weapons seen," came the dispatch over the cruiser radio. At the same time, a message, similar to an instant message on a smartphone, popped up on the MDT regarding the same call.

"Ten-four, Twenty-Five en route," Gerald said into the cruiser microphone. "Okay, Donna, here's your first code-three call." Gerald recited the three types of response codes. "Code one is routine response, no lights or siren, obey the traffic laws. Code two is more urgent, just the emergency lights, and you can suspend following traffic laws, but keep your speed close to the limit. Code three is urgent, lights and siren, drive as quickly and safely as possible, no need to obey traffic laws. Do you know where you're going?"

"I know it's in the Village, but I don't know exactly where the street is," Donna replied, trying not to sound too excited.

"Head toward the Village, and I'll guide you as we get closer. This is one of those times when you want to know where you're going without having to look it up or stare at the MDT. Go ahead and hit the lights and siren and pick up the pace."

Donna did as she was told, driving through two intersections against the light, which she later thought was fun only because she had never done it before. Long before they even got close to the address where the domestic was occurring, Gerald turned off the siren. "We don't want to warn them we're coming," Gerald said. "The lights will stay on 'til we get to the last corner, then all of them will be turned off."

Gerald and Donna could've pulled up to the address making all the noise possible, and it wouldn't have changed the beating that was occurring. On the open sidewalk, and easy to see as they covered the last fifty yards to the assault, were a man and a woman. She was on her back, lying on the ground with her arms crossed over her face. The man, on his knees, straddled her, pinning the smaller woman to the ground. She could not escape the furious beating of his fists. Whenever the woman moved her arms to protect her face, the man drove his fists into her stomach. When she tried to protect her stomach, her assailant smashed his fists into her nose, eyes, and mouth. She looked fatigued and unable to defend herself. The assailant, though bigger than the woman, was tiring too, his blows landing with less frequency. But his aim was still sharp as he drilled his last punches into the woman's nose.

"Pull right up on them. I don't want this guy to get a chance to run," Gerald instructed. Donna did as she was told. Gerald opened his door, exiting the cruiser before Donna had it in park. He scurried around the front fender toward the assailant, who continued to pound the woman slowly and steadily, oblivious to the approaching officers.

"Break it up, asshole!" Gerald yelled, grabbing the assailant by the neck from behind and pulling him straight back and down. The man's head bounced on the sidewalk.

Donna had the fleeting thought that maybe Gerald had slammed him too hard, but then the man yelled out, "Fuck you! You can't hit me!"

"Fuck you, I can!" Gerald kicked him in the chest to keep him down, simultaneously unsnapping his pepper spray from his duty belt and painting the man's face with the burning liquid. Gerald gave an extra special shot into the asshole's mouth at close range. It took about twenty seconds for the effects of the spray to grab hold, during which time Gerald kept kicking the assailant's arms and legs out from under him, keeping him off balance and on the ground. A late-arriving witness would think Gerald was beating a poor, defenseless man.

Finally, the wave of stinging pain from the pepper spray kicked in, and tears formed in the assailant's eyes, and mucus began to run from his nose and mouth. His eyes burned worse with each blink, the excruciating pinprick searing heat to his eyes and throat became overwhelming. He started to yelp in pain. Unconsciously, Donna smiled at the asshole's discomfort as Gerald forced the assailant onto his belly, handcuffing him and cinching the cuffs one or two clicks tighter than what was prescribed in the police officer's standards of training. Gerald left the man on the ground, writhing in pain from the pepper spray, and turned his attention to the woman who'd been attacked.

"Let's take a look at you, miss," Gerald said as he knelt next to her.

The woman had rolled up to a sitting position on the ground, her arms shaking. Crying now, almost hysterically, her words coming in fits, "I don't know why. . . . I don't know why. . . . I . . . I . . ."

Tears from both emotional and physical pain streamed out of eyes bruised from past assaults. Blood and snot oozed out her nose and mixed with the blood from her cut lips. The domestic casualty wiped her face, smearing the blood-snot goop across the back of her hand. Donna's first instinct would have been to put her arms around the woman and comfort her, then ask her why she stuck around this asshole. But with the high risk of contagious blood-borne pathogens, like hepatitis and HIV, Donna knew she didn't want any of this woman's blood on her uniform, never mind her skin. Donna knelt an arm's length away and donned the surgical rubber gloves all first responders carried. Then, not knowing what else to do, she held her hand.

In a low tone, Gerald instructed Donna. "Let's see if she can stand and try to get her into the house. Her neighbors watching this only makes it worse for her. I'll secure this asshole in the back of the cruiser and call for medical to check her out."

Donna guided the woman back inside her modest home while Gerald half-picked up, half-dragged the assailant to his feet. The pepper spray was doing its thing as the male screamed in garbled words, "I can't breathe—it burns—I can't breathe!"

"Shut the fuck up, you pussy," Gerald said into the assailant's ear, too softly for two witnesses across the street holding up their cell phones to hear. He knew the pain his arrestee was in, suffering the sensation of burning hot needles to the eyes and throat, having subjected himself to a full-on dose years earlier for a training video. "You're a tough guy when you beat a woman senseless, but now you're crying like a baby."

Gerald opened the door and, in an act of insincere compassion, placed the man in the back seat of the cruiser, being careful not to let his head hit the door frame. Gerald walked around to the driver's seat and closed the windows of the cruiser. The two witnesses, cell phones out in front of them, presumably in video recording mode, began walking toward the cruiser.

"Back up, guys," Gerald commanded. "Stay on the sidewalk." They reacted by stopping in the middle of the road and focusing their cell phones on Gerald. "You guys see what happened here?" He asked.

One witness grabbed and tugged on his crotch with one hand then stated, "No, they wasn't fightin' but you was beatin' on him, an I gots it on my phone. You gonna be on the news! Po Po gonna lose his job!"

"How about you two giving me your names and numbers, and I put you in as witnesses to be called to court to testify?" Gerald countered.

Almost in unison, the two witnesses clicked off their cell phones and placed them in their pockets. Gerald stepped toward them, and they retreated to the sidewalk, one of them yelling, "Yo don't need our names."

Gerald had played the game of whose dick is bigger since he was an adolescent boy, and these two locals were just the latest players to challenge him. Retreating to the front fender of his cruiser and leaning on it, Gerald hooked his thumbs into his gun belt, in a relaxed and non-aggressive pose. He knew two things could happen. A mob could suddenly show up to harass and bait him into a front-page newsworthy confrontation, or these two witnesses would get bored and leave him alone. Boredom was winning, and Gerald reasoned no one else was going to cause a problem. Any witness within eyesight had probably observed the beating the woman had taken and secretly sided with the cops.

Confident the scene would remain calm, Gerald opened the door of the cruiser and reached in for the AM/FM radio. He found a country music station and, as luck would have it, a Cody Johnson country song about dancing a woman home was playing. Gerald smiled and twisted up the volume knob. There couldn't have been a more appropriate song to fill this asshole's ears than one about a woman giving a guy half a chance at romance so he might dance her way home; much better than the vibrating gut-thumping rap songs about beating one's ho and bitch, the soundtrack of this neighborhood. Gerald opened the trunk and grabbed some written statement forms from his duty bag. Slamming the trunk shut, he could hear the painful wails of the assailant mixed with Cody's smooth voice from inside the cruiser. *Good times.*

A backup unit arrived, and Gerald asked them to keep

an eye on the prisoner while he checked on Donna and the female half of this domestic.

"She's calming down a bit," said Donna.

"I'll get a quick statement from her. I forgot the camera. Can you get it for me? It's in my duty bag, outside right pocket. We can take pictures of her injuries while they're still bloody; it'll make more of an impact when he goes to court Monday morning."

Donna left, and Gerald asked the woman her name and if she lived here. Always start with the easy questions first, get the victim to start talking. Her name was Luanne and, yes, she lives here. Gerald moved on to the next question: What had happened? From experience, he already knew what had occurred in the house that evening. He could've written the whole report five seconds after arriving. All domestics were the same.

There was always the abuser—usually the male half, but not always—who had to be in charge. It was always about control, and the victims all shared the same trait: lack of self-esteem. Sometimes a huge lack, sometimes just enough. But it was the common ingredient. The abusers expertly played off their partners' weakness, telling them they were beautiful until they punched them, loving them sweetly until they called them stupid and punched them, spending money extravagantly and then blaming the victim for money woes and punching them, demanding loyalty while they themselves lacked fidelity and then raping and punching them. The victims stuck around out of real fear, the abuser sometimes threatening to kill them if they tried to leave. An empty lot just three doors down was a reminder; the threat to kill is sometimes real. In that case, the abuser had been court-ordered out of the family home and figured if he couldn't live with his family, no one would. The asshole killed his wife and two daughters before burning the bodies to ashes and the house to the ground.

Today Gerald knew he was about to get a good story,

and the truth, from the woman. He called it the "scared shitless syndrome." *The closer a person is in time to having been scared shitless, the closer they are to telling the truth about what happened.* In this case, Gerald surmised there was little time for thoughts of blind love, family obligations, lack of money, shame, or isolation from family to mellow the woman's story in her assailant's favor.

Gerald didn't take out his notepad and pen yet. He just wanted to get this abused woman, Luanne, to talk freely. She did. Luanne explained to Gerald what had happened: She'd refused to have sex because her man stuck his dick in another woman.

Good times. "Um, you're going to have to explain this a little more."

Luanne stared at the floor with slumped shoulders wishing all of this would go away. Suddenly straightening her back, she looked Gerald straight in the eyes and began talking, her words gushing out in one long sentence, "He stay out all night last night just getting home now, almost twenty-four hour later? He give me some bullshit 'bout drinkin' too much an stayin' at a friend's house, but I knows better and pulled down his pants and smell his dick and it smell like pussy so I know he fucked someone else last night and I tell him he too stupid to even wash his dick off then he hit me an' didn't stop hittin' me till you show up."

"Okay," said Gerald, "you caught him cheating on you, you called him on it, and then he beat you up."

"Yeah, an' he think I cheatin' on him, but I don't. I love him." Then she turned to face out the door and yelled, "I used to love him."

She isn't scared, thought Gerald, *she called him out on his cheating, took the punches, and isn't backing down. Tough lady.* Gerald wrote down what Luanne said, just the way she'd said it, with the incorrect tenses and other violations of the English language, on the statement form. "Okay, Luanne, will you read this statement and sign the bottom?"

She shook her head. "No, no, no, ain't signin' nothin'. I just don't want him to come back."

"How long have you two lived together?"

"Six months."

"Well, if you *don't* sign, there's a better chance of him coming back than if you *do* sign it. We can add in there that you don't ever want him to come back. Will you sign it then?"

Luanne agreed.

"The medics are here, Luanne. They'll try to clean up those wounds, but first, let us take a couple of pictures for the report," Gerald said.

The paramedics had arrived on their fire truck, and an ambulance with its two-person crew, there to transport Luanne if she needed it, was also parked outside. Gerald looked around for a second. Three cops, Gerald, Donna, and their backup, three firefighters (two paramedics and a driver), and two EMTs on the ambulance. Eight first responders to a routine domestic. A generation ago, if someone called in something like this, one or two cops might've been dispatched, and there was a good chance they would've decided it was a private family affair and not made an arrest.

That had changed in Connecticut after the Tracey Thurman case in 1983. Tracey, then twenty-two, had suffered ongoing physical abuse from her husband, Charles "Buck" Thurman, who was also the father of their two-year-old child. On June tenth, Buck again started assaulting Tracey at their Torrington home, and she called the police. They took more than twenty minutes to arrive, despite numerous restraining orders and complaints of abuse Tracey had brought to the attention of police. In between the call to the police and their arrival, Buck stabbed Tracey thirteen times in the neck, shoulders, and face. Tracey survived, spending seven months in the hospital. The results of her injuries

39

were loss of tactile feel on one side of her body and eighty percent loss of motor skills on the other.

She sued the Town of Torrington, stating that her constitutional rights to equal protection guaranteed under the Fourteenth Amendment had been violated. At the time, the prevailing thought—if not direct policy—of the police and courts was not to arrest violent and abusive husbands. Beating one's wife was a family issue, not a criminal one. Tracey argued, and won, on the grounds that victims of assaults and abuse outside of a domestic relationship were afforded more protection than those victims who suffered assaults and abuse from within one.

As a result of losing the lawsuit, the State of Connecticut had passed the Thurman Act, making domestic violence an act warranting an immediate arrest regardless of whether the victim wanted to press charges.

As Gerald and Donna climbed back into their cruiser, the medics were trying to convince a reluctant Luanne to go to the hospital and have her injuries examined, explaining in the simplest terms what a concussion is and why she should be evaluated. Their arrestee, now identified as Reginald Timms, squirmed and cried in the backseat. It had been a full ten minutes since he had been sprayed, and it would be another ten to twenty before the effects started to wear off. Gerald turned off the AM/FM radio and announced to dispatch that they were coming in with one prisoner. Donna started to roll down her window, but Gerald asked her to keep it closed. "A fresh-air breeze is the antidote, so to speak, for pepper spray. Let him suffer a little more with the windows closed on the drive. Once we get there, we'll let him rinse his eyes out with cold water. Make it look good for the cameras in the booking room should he want to make a complaint." Gerald spoke quietly, trying to keep Reginald from hearing the conversation over his own cries.

During the short drive to headquarters, Reginald cried, pleading for the officers to stop the burning pain. Neither

Gerald nor Donna said anything. They exchanged a glance once after a particularly loud cry from the cage. Gerald mouthed *pussy* and looked away. Donna shrugged her shoulders slightly and continued driving. *Fuck you, Reginald.*

Reginald was booked and processed with little difficulty. Afterward, at a round table in the break room where conspicuous signs to keep the sink and microwave clean are ignored, Gerald reviewed with Donna how to document the incident. "We need to fill out a domestic violence form, the report itself, and a use-of-force form. Actually, *I* have to do all of this."

"Why three forms? Aren't all the questions answered in the arrest report?"

"Well, the first form is for the state; they need to know about all domestic violence incidents. The use-of-force form is just for the department to keep track of how we lump up our arrestees. You'll catch more crap from your boss for not filling out a form correctly or forgetting to turn one in than anything else. Deputy Chief Neaballa, aka No Balls, has actually said on several occasions that the best skill a cop can have is typing. No lie. And I say that not just to bust the DC's balls, but to let you know where the administration places their values. They couldn't care less that we just saved a woman from being beaten more than she was. Miss a block on that domestic violence form a few times, and your reputation as a cop, in the administration's eyes, will be that you're incompetent or lazy. But that's another lesson for another day. Let's debrief the domestic we just had while it's still fresh in our heads."

After reviewing the domestic incident and how they, as officers, reacted, Gerald put Donna on the spot. "If you'd arrived by yourself, and backup wasn't there yet, what would you have done to break up the fight—to keep the woman from being beaten anymore?"

"I guess I would have done what you did: pepper spray him," Donna answered.

"But the pepper spray took twenty seconds to take effect. I've seen it take a full minute on people under the influence of crack and alcohol. You into martial arts fighting, or UFC stuff?"

"No, just what I learned at the academy."

"Ever been punched in the face? Got into a real fight with an adult? Schoolyard shit doesn't count."

"No."

"I have two experiences here for you. First, years ago, we used to teach defensive tactics, the cop version of self-defense, here at the police department. At the end of the day, the instructors would get volunteers to do what they called the 'fight for life,' in which an officer would volunteer to perform a full sixty seconds of all-out punching, kicking, and pounding of an instructor wearing a padded suit. At the sixty-second mark, the officer would have to get the instructor into handcuffs. You know what we found out?"

"What?"

"That most officers, of either gender, had about twenty-five to thirty seconds of energy to fight full-on against an opponent. Remember, this is simulated street fighting, not a paced boxing or wrestling match. In the second half of their 'fight for life,' their legs became leaden, their arms heavy and hard to move. They were completely out of breath. Some guys came close to passing out. The blows they landed were ineffective. In the initial seconds of a fight, you stop breathing—you're holding your breath, like when you try to lift a heavy piece of furniture. Obviously, that's counterproductive to being a good fighter, and contributes to the officer losing energy—therefore power—and feeling dizzy. The guys who fared the best were former high school wrestlers and martial arts guys. They were tired, but still effective at the end. They've trained, to some degree, to breathe during a fight. The runners and cyclists did okay, but endurance breathing and getting your rate of respiration under control in a fight are two different things. The rest of the cops—the majority—were not in any real physical shape to effectively go a full sixty seconds. And some, like me, are getting into our forties, and the physical conditioning we had in our twenties or thirties just isn't going to happen for most of us now. But the instructors chose sixty seconds because, like I said, it takes nearly that long for pepper spray to take effect on an asshole who's drunk or high on cocaine. In fact, if they *are* high, they won't really feel the pain, but eventually will have a hard time seeing through watery eyes. They'll still fight, just blindly."

Donna nodded, understanding the point Gerald was making, but she believed she could handle herself in physical confrontation even though she had never been in a physical fight in her life.

"Second story. I'm a new cop, maybe a year on the job, working midnights, and I'm parked by the Burnside/Hillside intersection filling out a report when I hear glass breaking and a lot of shouting. About three buildings down is a neighborhood bar, and it looked like a fight had spilled into the street. It wasn't uncommon for that bar on a weekend night, so I roll into the middle of the fight with my cruiser and call dispatch, which at the same time was getting a 911 call from the bar.

"Now, most times when breaking up a bar fight, the spectators will quickly disperse when the cops show up, and it's easy to see who's doing the fighting. In this case, the crowd did scatter, but the main combatant, one Michael Deluco, wasn't fighting one guy. He was there to fight everyone. I knew Michael from previous encounters, and he generally cooperated with me. He was about my size with just a little heavier build. So this time, he started out cooperating. I easily guided him away from the crowd toward my cruiser by just holding his arm. About three steps from the cruiser, he spins, picks me completely off the ground, horizontal, and slams me down, gun-side up. At that time, I weighed about one hundred and ninety pounds in full uniform and gear. I got slammed like a rag doll. My only thought, as I'm staring at the dirt and grass in front of my face, is to protect the gun—if he gets to it, he'll kill me. Reflexively, just like I was trained to do, I place both hands over the gun and holster and expect to get the shit kicked out of me.

"Fortunately for me, Deluco decided to run instead of fight. Also, someone from the bar again called 911 to let them know, 'One of your officers is getting the shit beat out of him.' This got our entire squad, plus a few leftover guys from evening shift, to come to my rescue. I get up and start running after Deluco. He made it about a hundred yards before he ran out of breath. About that time, backup cruisers were arriving, and I tell you, when you're in a real fight and scared, there's nothing better to see and hear than the lights and sirens of your brother officers screaming up the road to save your ass.

"After a couple of minutes, there's eight or nine of us, our whole squad, in the middle of the street just trying to get Deluco handcuffed and into the back of a cruiser. He wouldn't budge. He just stiffened up and stood there, a solid block of muscle. We couldn't bend his arms or knees, couldn't knock him down. We didn't have pepper spray or Tasers back then. Just PR-24s and nightsticks, which we were using like Mexicans on a piñata. At the time, we kinda assumed he was under the influence of cocaine because he ain't feeling a thing. We were actually getting tired. It's taking a lot more than sixty seconds to get this guy secured—we were into several minutes now—and all of us are getting out of breath.

"It's almost comical thinking about it now, but two guys would go in and beat on him, get tired, then two other guys would take over. We used the nightsticks on his shins . . . full baseball hitter swings. Nothing was registering as pain on Deluco. Shins, knees, forearms, everything but his head and torso, over and over with the nightsticks. We finally get him, so he's between the open back door and body of a cruiser, but we can't bend his body enough to get him in. One of our guys gets in from the other side and starts pulling on his waist, and I get a running start and do a flying kick into Deluco's gut from the opposite side to finally bend him enough to stuff him in the cage. He's not handcuffed, so he's just going nuts in the back of the cruiser, kicking at the windows, which prisoners have smashed out with their feet or heads, so it's a code-three run the three blocks to the PD, where the evening shift leftovers are primed, fresh and ready to deliver whatever force needed to control Deluco as they moved him from the cruiser to the cellblock.

"The next morning, maybe six hours after the fight, I go to process him, and I'm a little nervous, even though there are maybe five of us surrounding Deluco when I fingerprint him. But he was cooperative and admitted he'd done coke and drank brandy before the bar fight. It was also obvious in the light of day how super jacked-up he was, muscle-wise. He'd come out of prison a week earlier after doing six months for assault, and he said he worked out every day."

Gerald paused, shaking his head. "I went home that day for the first time realizing that I was vulnerable as a street cop. Up until that incident, I'd always come out on top, either through good talk or physical strength. But Deluco, in his coke-and-alcohol-fueled state, could've easily beaten me to death if he chose to. And if Deluco had made that choice, I would've had to shoot him, if able, to save myself. I look at the Michael Brown case—he's the guy the cop shot in Ferguson, Missouri—and see the similarities. Only difference is Deluco ran away, and Brown was going back to beat the cop some more."

Gerald stared blankly for a few moments at the microwave. The Deluco fight years ago had permanently altered how he went about police work. He didn't see Deluco's body slam coming. He had missed the signs of an imminent assault on him, and it could have cost him dearly. Never again. He began to consciously hone his observations of people on the street. Their hands, their eyes, the position of their feet, the rotation of their head, words they used. Fight, flight, posturing, or complete cooperation are the four options a suspect has with the police. Gerald learned to talk down the most highly agitated. Just because a guy is punching holes in his walls doesn't mean he's going to punch you. However, a suspect appearing calm but repeatedly pulling up his pants—Are his pants loose, or is he trying to adjust a weapon concealed in his waistband?— can lull you into a false sense of security. That suspect is less obvious but maybe more dangerous than a wall puncher. Gerald started to observe the old-timers, the road warriors who had been in patrol their entire career, how they could appear to relate to any potential assailant, get them to run out of mental and emotional gas, but be hair-trigger ready to hit them first and fuck them up just enough so they don't or can't fight you. Every street encounter was different and often boring, but to Gerald, it was always an opportunity to assess and hone his body language skills. He had been the subject of numerous use-of-force complaints, maybe a little more than other officers. But he also had gone home every night with barely a scratch on him, a win in his mind.

Gerald focused his eyes on Donna and attempted to put his experience into words of wisdom for her. "You have to understand—and get this very clear in your head—that there's a distinction between violence and brutality. Violence of action, as the SWAT guys say, is what keeps the good guys alive. It's a part of police work, a very small part, but it's the part that separates us from every other social worker out there. Maybe one to two percent of your work time, you have to use violence. And you have to be absolutely correct when you do. Brutality is abusing a person to get your rocks off. Totally immoral. Like in ancient Rome, when Saint Peter is being led to a dungeon to await his execution and some soldier smashed Peter's head into the stone wall so hard it left an indentation in the stone." Donna furrowed her brow, giving him a quizzical look.

"True story, look it up under Mamertine Prison. Anyway, as the story is told, that's an example of brutality, though I would be curious to hear the soldier's point of view. We will never know if maybe Peter tried to kick the soldier in the balls or told him to fuck off one too many times, and the soldier snapped."

Donna slid her phone out from her back pocket and started to peck at it with one finger. Gerald said, "Let me finish my little lecture here before you Google Saint Peter's stone-denting head." Donna placed her phone face down on the table. "In the police world, walking the line between violence and brutality is you, the cop, establishing and maintaining your own street cred."

"Not sure what you mean by walking the line?" said Donna.

"Over here, on the one hand," Gerald said, fully extending his left arm, "are some cops who aren't going to put a hand on anyone no matter what. They're reluctant to use violence, even when the situation requires it. According to the FBI, which tracks law enforcement line-of-duty deaths, a large percentage of cops killed waited too long to defend themselves. Over here, on the other hand"—Gerald's right arm reached out—"are other cops who jump into violence too soon or escalate a situation because they're lazy, or have poor people skills, or they just want to prove how tough they are by knocking someone down, and they end up injuring a citizen, or worse.

"People on the street will know pretty quickly how you handle yourself. Are you letting people walk all over you? Avoiding confrontation? Not good—no street cred." Gerald shook his left hand. "Are you lumping people up when you shouldn't? Body-slamming or punching someone when it's not necessary? That's not good either. You'll be known on the street as a knuckle dragger with no brains, and people with no brains aren't trusted by anyone—including your colleagues in the locker room." Gerald shook his right hand. "We're lucky in this department that it's hard to find anyone working here at either extreme, but there are degrees in between where all cops fall."

Gerald checked some boxes on the use-of-force form. "Then there's the personal part of it. Asshole punches me, I'm going off on him. Drunk driver runs me off the road and, after I catch up and pull him over, I'll watch him do a face-plant when he loses his balance in his attempt to perform the field sobriety tests. Asshole runs from me, I'm gonna catch up and tackle him. If he's punching, kicking, and scratching me to get away . . . fuck that. I'm not a punching bag, and I'm not here to get hurt, but I *am* here to hurt you for trying to fuck me up, and sometimes there might be a few extra punches to the kidneys or an extra click or two with the cuffs. Whether that enhances or detracts from my street cred with the criminals, I don't know—nor do I care. But I'll say this: once you've been beat up, or one of your squadmates ends up in the hospital because they got worked over, it'll change your mind by a few degrees what you consider justified violence versus brutality."

To Donna, it was beginning to sound like Gerald was trying to justify how he'd handled Reggie earlier. She decided just to stay quiet. Gerald felt like he was failing in getting his point across and found himself thinking, *How do you simulate getting the shit kicked out of you to a trainee?*

"I'll sum it up. Deluco always respected me after that night. He would fuck with other cops but not with me."

Gerald went back to the earlier domestic. "So, back to the original question. How would you handle this evening's assailant if you were by yourself?"

"Pepper spray and maybe my Taser," said Donna.

"And lots of verbal commands," Gerald added. "*Loud* verbal commands. Bellowing out your orders does help to sensory overload some assholes sometimes, but more importantly, it's what the witnesses will hear and record on their phones."

His phone went off as he and Donna were finishing the last of the paperwork. It was the desk sergeant, Sergeant Onslow. "Hey, Gerald, you have calls holding for you. Are you getting back on the road soon?"

"Heading out now, Sarge. Have dispatch send the calls to my MDT." Gerald clicked off his phone and said to Donna, "Some supervisors, like Sergeant Onslow, keep checking their screen to see how long their people are on calls. If he thinks you are taking too long, he gives you a little hint to move along. That phone call was a hint, so let's go."

Back in their cruiser, Donna turned the key to the ignition and stared at the MDT screen displaying a small stack of calls waiting for their attention. Buckling in, she smiled and said, "Your story about Saint Peter, does that mean I have to worry about encountering future saints on the street?"

Gerald grinned. "Not in this town."

5

Friday
June 9
1303 hours

DONNA PARKED THE CRUISER IN front of the main doors to the high school, a structure built in the mid-1970s that housed the 1,700 students plus faculty and administrators and two school resource police officers (SROs). She and Gerald walked past the main offices and trophy case at the front of the lobby and made a right turn down a locker-lined hallway that was nearly one hundred yards long. Ahead of them were two black female students slowly walking toward each other from opposite directions. Just as they passed each other one turned to the other and yelled out, "Yo legs is fat!"

The second student then turned to the first and replied, "That's from sittin' down on black dick!" as she squatted and mimed the motion she was describing. Both girls cackled and continued on their way.

Gerald smiled, thinking to himself, *Kids like this keep us employed.* Donna worked to keep a stoic face.

Donna and Gerald finally came to a small door that had a sign over it, displaying the words school resource officer. The door was open slightly, and the light was on inside as Gerald knocked and gently pushed the door open until it stopped against the knee of a fourteen-year-old girl sitting on a plastic chair behind the door. Gerald peered around the door at the girl who didn't look up at him but stared sullenly at the back of the door. Her hands were on her lap and handcuffed. Gerald turned and looked at Officer Pete Slisz, who was sitting at a desk, actually a card table being used as a desk, and asked, "You need a transport?"

Pete turned and smiled. "Hi, Gerald. Welcome to my office. Like what I've done to the place? It used to be a utility closet, but now I've got a table, chair, and computer. All the tools I need to do police work."

Gerald smiled slightly and took a step back, allowing Donna the chance to step up and glance around Pete's office. Donna and Pete introduced themselves to each other, and then Pete explained that he needed the fourteen-year-old brought to headquarters and locked up in the juvenile cell.

"What's her offense?" Gerald asked.

"She got into a pretty good fight with another girl," Pete said, nodding toward the juvenile. "She'll be charged with assault third. She was hair pulling and throwing some pretty good punches to the face of another girl, causing a bloody nose and probably a headache. My partner is with the other girl in the nurse's office, waiting for her parents to come down. This one won't talk to me or anyone else, and I can't get a hold of her mother, so it's off to jail for her for a few hours."

Pete quickly wrote the juvenile's information on his notepad, tore off the piece of paper and handed it to Gerald, and said, "Here you go. I'll be in shortly to process her. If you could just have Donna pat her down before securing her in a cell and fill in the log at the watch commander's desk, I'd greatly appreciate it."

"No problem," Gerald said. Then, turning to Donna, he said, "Before we go, I want you to re-do the cuffs behind her back and give her a good pat-down." Donna did as she was asked and began escorting the juvenile down the long hall.

Once Donna was a few feet away, Pete called to Gerald, who turned back. "Get a load of this," Pete said. "The administration sent me a memo stating they want me to show more 'parity' in juvenile arrests and referrals, which is a thinly veiled order to make fewer arrests of minorities. I sent a response saying I'll make sure to arrest and refer fewer Asian and Indian kids. They didn't find any humor in that." Gerald smiled and nodded. Pete had always had a sharp wit about him.

Gerald said, "You're here to serve the kids first and the politicians and administration second. I would keep doing what you're doing. I know the kids in this school have a tremendous amount of respect for you, Pete, at least you have that going for you."

"Thanks, Gerald, that's good to hear. And thanks for taking that juvy in, I'll be there in about a half-hour to process her."

"No problem."

Fifteen minutes later, Donna came up from the cellblock to meet Gerald at the watch commander's desk. "She's in her cell," Donna said.

"Good," said Gerald. "I've got her logged in. I just have to find the desk sergeant to make sure he knows Pete will be in soon to finish processing her. Otherwise, he'll think the juvenile is our responsibility and start barking at us for not having all the paperwork done." Gerald disappeared, leaving Donna to stand by herself.

Donna scanned the office and noticed a three-inch binder labeled "memos" and wondered why in the age of electronic documents, there was a binder of hard-copied memorandums. She was thinking, *Just look them up on the computer,* when she heard a shriek down the hall. Not the kind of shriek of pain or fear but the ear-piercing kind only kids can make when they are excited. The shriek was followed by the combined sound of small feet running and larger feet thumping down the hall toward her. Donna stepped out into the hallway. *Could this be a foot chase inside the PD? I'm in on this!*

She was met by a boy who looked to be about seven years old and went from running to a full stop in front of her with a squeal from his sneakers. The boy looked up and smiled at Donna, then started vigorously shaking a full bottle of soda. Watch Commander Sergeant Glenn Onslow and Gerald, who had been a few steps behind the boy, caught up and stopped.

"Whoa, hey, Cory, that's not such a good idea," Glenn said as he reached over Cory's head, relieving him of the soda bottle.

"Who is this?" Donna asked.

"This is Cory. He's come to visit us for a little bit." Then turning to Cory, Glenn said, "Why don't you watch the TV across the hall with the other officers for a minute?"

Cory replied, "Okay," with a smile and scurried across the hall.

Glenn motioned for Gerald and Donna to follow him into the watch commander's office. "Close the door," Glenn said as he sat down behind his desk. "We got a call about two hours ago regarding an unresponsive female in an apartment down the street. How it all came about is a friend came to visit the apartment. Cory lets them in, and the friend looks around for Cory's mom and finds her unresponsive on her bed. We get the call and send medics and an officer. Medics get there, check on Cory's thirty-six-year-old mom, determine she's dead, and leave. Through all this, Cory doesn't know his mom is dead. The officer on scene and the friend who came to visit were quick enough to keep Cory occupied while the medics were there. Before Cory could figure anything out, we drove him here and called the Department of Children and Families."

"Are we still waiting for DCF?" asked Gerald.

"No," Glenn continued, "they are here interviewing next of kin to determine if any of them are fit enough to take temporary custody of Cory. In the meantime, we are babysitting Cory, and I have an officer and a detective at the apartment waiting for the medical examiner to arrive."

"Is the death suspicious?"

"Only in that the woman is young. Could be a natural death, suicide, or overdose. Time will tell."

At that moment, the office door swung open, and Cory sped into the room and said, "I'm done watching TV!" Cory smiled and looked back and forth between Donna Gerald and Glenn.

Gerald said, "Cory, have you had anything to eat lately?"

Cory enthusiastically nodded his head as Glenn said, "The guys have bought him McDonald's, candy bars, and, as you can probably tell, several sodas."

Gerald looked at Cory, into his eyes and at his smile. The kid seemed genuinely happy. Gerald then noticed Cory's T-shirt, which had, "If you think I'm cute you should see my mother," written in goofy letters printed across the front of it. Gerald smiled at the irony. *Your mother is dead and being stuffed into a body bag as we speak, kid,* he thought, *she ain't pretty no more.* Gerald's heart suddenly grew heavy. Cory's bright eyes and smile hadn't diminished. He didn't know his mom was dead. Glenn and the rest of the officers were helping him live a few more moments of happiness before he would be told the dreadful news.

"Gerald, if you and your new rider here could watch after Cory for a while, that would be great."

Gerald smiled, trying to project more enthusiasm than he felt, and said, "Sure, we can watch him. We can walk across the parking lot and visit the fireman and play on their trucks. How does that sound, Cory?"

Cory hopped up and down and replied, "Yesss."

Glenn said, "I have to catch up on my paperwork and deal with the lady in the lobby who feels she didn't deserve the traffic ticket she got this morning. DCF is in interview room two talking to Cory's uncle and aunt. Hopefully, it won't be too much longer."

Donna opened the back door of the headquarters building, and Cory started to sprint past her. "Hold on, Cory," Gerald shouted, "you have to hold our hands crossing the parking lot. We don't want you getting hit by a car." Cory stopped and reached up for both Gerald's and Donna's hands. *Total trust*, thought Gerald.

Gerald turned his head to Donna as they walked with Cory between them and said, "You may or may not have picked up on it, but Glenn is old school in some ways."

"You mean by calling me 'your rider' instead of my name?"

"Yeah, that and assuming you have maternal instincts."

"Uh-huh."

"Some old-timers came on the job when the senior guys didn't talk to the rookies for a year. Kind of an initiation process in their minds. That's why he called you 'my rider.' He also thinks women are better than men at taking care of children. He saw you in the hallway, and it was 'problem solved' with regard to our friend here."

"Not calling me by name doesn't bother me, but the assumption that I know how to take care of a child is idiotic. I'm not really sure I know how to keep Cory entertained."

"It's easy. Watch." As the three reached the edge of the parking lot, Gerald asked Cory, "Do you see that big bell by the firehouse?"

"Yes," Cory replied.

"Go over and pull on the rope attached to it as hard as you can. It will make the bell ring. See how loud you can make it ring."

Cory let go of their hands and sprinted the ten yards across the manicured lawn to the bell, an old bell removed from a firehouse facing demolition years earlier and mounted on a cement pedestal. Cory rang the bell.

"Louder," Gerald shouted, encouraging Cory.

"Won't the firemen find this annoying?" Donna asked after a full minute of bell ringing.

"Yup, especially the deputy fire chief who is an old neighbor of mine and whose window is on the second floor right over the bell," Gerald said with a smile.

CLANG, CLANG, CLANG.

6

Saturday
July 8
1320 hours

GERALD DENNEN DROPPED HIS PACK and looked up at the old fire tower on the summit of Mount Carrigain. Going for a hike had not been in his plans, but yesterday his live-in girlfriend, Emily, had decided at the last minute that they should drive from Connecticut to the Presidential mountain range in New Hampshire and hike the Nancy Pond loop, a two-day walk through the woods and hills. Gerald reasoned good times often come from last-minute plans and set up their backpacks.

They had left his condo early, 0500, with their backpacks full of gear for an overnight hike and loaded into the back of Emily's Subaru Forester. Four and a half hours later, they parked in a dirt parking lot next to one of the trailheads. The air was warm but dry in the White Mountains of New Hampshire, a comfortable respite from the humidity blanketing southern New England.

They had started out hiking together at the same pace, but after an hour, Gerald was more than a half-mile ahead of Emily. Once the trail got steep going up the mountain, the gap between them increased. Gerald still had a working man's strength left over from the years he worked construction. Though of average height, he was just "thicker," as one of his co-workers put it: thick fingers, forearms, and legs. His cardio conditioning wasn't as ample as his raw strength, so he had to stop to catch his breath more than he felt he should have, but even still, the gap between him and Emily increased.

Gerald ascended into the thickening overcast, hiking up through the cloud layer into the brilliant sunshine. Now, at the top of the mountain and above the clouds, the view was clear in all directions. Mount Washington, the most famous of the Presidentials, could be seen to the north. Gerald decided to wait for Emily before climbing the fire tower to take in the view from the top. He wasn't sure if she would be pissed that he had gone ahead of her or content being on the trail on her own.

Emily was five-foot-three and appeared to exercise regularly, but, in reality, didn't. She was a voracious reader of everything from cheap romance novels to law journals, and given the option of reading or working up a sweat in the mountains of New Hampshire, she would have chosen perusing a book. But hiking was an activity she could do with Gerald, who usually paced himself ahead of her then patiently waited at trail intersections or summits for her to catch up. They were separate but together, sharing the same experience. The evening hours at a campsite with Gerald after a day's hike was what she took the most pleasure in. The contentment after a day of physical work combined with the simplicity of a warm meal, simple shelter, and time with Gerald without distractions was her reward.

Gerald and Emily had been together for just over two years. They had met at a charity motorcycle ride for disabled veterans. He had ridden his Harley-Davidson Road King to the parking lot where the riders were assembling, paid his donation, and searched out some coffee. Emily had volunteered to work the snack tent with one of her girlfriends who kept badgering her to get her nose out of a book and socialize more.

A line had formed at the snack tent, and Gerald waited

patiently while judging the custom work on other bikes, mentally assessing what might look good on his. When it was his turn to order, it was Emily who had waited on him and retrieved his coffee, black no sugar. As she counted out his change, Emily smiled and asked Gerald what the symbol, a blue line through a silhouette of the American flag on the front of his black T-shirt stood for.

"It represents the thin blue line," Gerald had said. Emily just smiled and nodded; Gerald wasn't sure she knew what he meant. "It represents police officers as the line between what's bad in this world and what's good."

"Are you a police officer or a supporter of law enforcement?"

Gerald smiled, "I'm both." He then gestured with his coffee toward Emily's University of Connecticut T-shirt and asked, "Are you a student or a fan of UConn's sports teams?"

"I'm both. I'm studying law at UConn," Emily said.

"You want to be a prosecutor or defense attorney or one who files lawsuits?"

"Haven't decided."

"Do you like to ride motorcycles?"

"I don't know. I've never ridden on one before."

"My bike is over there by the grass. Dark red with an eagle pained in the tank. If you want to ride on the back, meet me there when the ride starts. I have a helmet you can use if you want."

"There's a chance I might do that."

Gerald smiled and walked back to his bike while carefully sipping his coffee. His current girlfriend had decided to stay home, claiming not to feel well, and Gerald had been content to leave her there. She was attractive and great in bed, but lately, she had been bringing up the topic of children more and more. *Time to get a new girlfriend. Maybe this coffee chick will come for a ride. She's pretty, friendly, and probably smart if she's studying law, though she's shorter than what I like in a woman.*

Emily did ride with Gerald that day, and they'd been

together ever since. Emily graduated and passed the bar exam. Now she was working for a law firm in Hartford, putting in long hours as a junior associate.

Gerald had found himself wanting to spend more time with her as their relationship grew, but she had spent a great deal of time studying for her law classes, then studying for the bar exam. And now she was working long hours five days a week and nearly a full day on weekends helping the partners and senior associates prepare cases. He was surprised Emily had suggested at the last minute to go on this overnight hike. Now he waited at the top of Mount Carrigain with some anxiety. *Is she enjoying herself or just going through the motions to keep me quiet?*

Twenty-five minutes later, Emily emerged from the trees into the small clearing. Gerald eyed her, looking for signs of fatigue, knowing frustration will follow after a certain point. The sweat stains showing on her long-sleeve T-shirt bled down onto the top of her leggings or yoga pants or whatever chicks called them. She was also out of breath but smiling.

Whew, thought Gerald as he admired the form of her shape in the yoga pants, *she looks like she's in a good mood.* "Not bad," Gerald said. "You're only a few minutes behind me."

"My legs feel rubbery, and I'm a little out of breath, but the views just back a little way are fantastic," Emily said.

"Here, let me grab your pack while you catch your breath. Then we can go to the top of the fire tower where the view will be even better," Gerald said as he helped Emily out of her pack and fetched her one of his full water bottles. She started drinking right away.

"You should probably get yourself a dry shirt for the hike down to the campsite. It's going to be cooler with the sun going behind the mountains." Emily nodded as she tipped a water bottle high to her mouth, getting the last drops from it.

Strength returned to Emily's legs as she climbed the steps

behind Gerald to the viewing platform at the top of the fire tower. Below them to the east was a cloud layer that went to the horizon. Lumpy and white, it appeared solid, as if you could walk on it. To the west were the ripples of mountain peaks layered into the distance without a cloud in sight. In between was the spine of the mountains that they were now on top of. Neither of them said any words as they shifted from one side of the platform to the other taking in the view, comfortable in each other's silence and shared experience.

Before descending the tower, they took a selfie together with the clouds to the east as a background. Gerald took some more pictures with his camera phone, trying to capture the beauty of the view, knowing the pictures wouldn't be of great quality but would serve as a special reminder of this hike with Emily. There was a wobbling fatigue in Emily's legs as she climbed down the steps, reminding her that going down a mountain can be just as much work as going up.

For the remainder of the day, they descended the mountain trail to a streamside campsite. With little difficulty, they located a flat spot to pitch their tent. Once they sorted their gear, Gerald squatted down and started heating their freeze-dried dinner over a tiny camping stove. Emily sat down next to him, letting out a grunt as her ass hit the ground. "I'm not sure I will be able to move in the morning," she said.

"There's some Advil in my pack plus a pint of Jack. Either one or both should help with the pain," said Gerald.

"I'll take some Advil before we go to sleep." Emily stared at Gerald for a few moments and, sliding herself a little closer to him, asked, "What were you thinking about all day?"

Gerald had heard this question, in different forms, from every girl he had dated going back to college, and his knee-jerk reaction was always, *None of your fucking business. If I wanted to let you in on what I'm thinking about, I would open my mouth and tell you.* Somewhere along the way among the many relationships he had with women, he finally discovered that it was the chick way of fishing for a compliment—*How great you look in that dress*—or a status on their relationship—*Just thinking about how much I love you*. Emily didn't play games with their relationship, and her thought process was generally deeper than most of the people Gerald hung out with. In a way, this intimidated him. Gerald took the simple route and was completely honest. "I was thinking of how great your ass looks in those leggings you hike in."

"Bullshit, you were ahead of me all day, and my ass is getting bigger with all the sitting I do nowadays."

"True. . . . Mostly I was thinking about taking the sergeant's test that's coming up."

"You should! I think you would make a wonderful sergeant. What's involved with the test?"

"The test itself is in two parts, a hundred-question written portion and an oral board comprised of a panel of higher-ranking officers from other police departments. Our administration has a formula to combine the grades from the two portions to give your final score. Any college degree that you have, regardless of what the degree is for, gives you a full point. Then you are ranked by your score. The difference between first and sixth can be as little as two points, so it's a tight race, especially when they only plan on promoting four people, and there's usually ten to twenty who take the test."

"Sounds fair enough. What about job performance? Any points for that?"

"As in an official review and rating of how good or bad an officer is and applying it to the final score?"

"Yeah."

"Not in my PD. There are no official reviews. You are either someone the administration likes, doesn't like, or doesn't know much about. If they like you, you can do no wrong. If they don't, you can do no right, and if they don't know you, then they will try to ask around, and any rumors about you, good or bad, become your reputation."

"Sounds very juvenile."

"It is. To compound the problem, backstabbing starts. I have seen guys who were friends screw each other over, right out in the open, to gain favor in the eyes of the admin around promotion time."

They were both quiet for a few moments, staring at the food that was starting to sizzle in the small aluminum pan. Emily said, "Two things. First, if you don't take it, then you can't complain about how things are run at the PD. At least if you are a sergeant, you can be in charge of a squad or investigations, right? A sergeant can try to influence things at some level, right?"

"True."

"And second, can you really tell that my ass is getting bigger?"

"You said yourself you sit around too much. But it's okay, gives me more woman to love."

Emily stood and pushed the still-squatting Gerald onto his back and said, "You're a jackass."

"Yes, I am," Gerald said as he rolled back up to a squat. "But you still get points for a nice rack."

"God . . ." Emily muttered as she crawled into the small tent to find the bottle of Jack.

As the campsite grew darker and cooler, Gerald and Emily finished their meals. Gerald made a bear bag containing their food and trash, attached a line to it, and slung it over a high tree branch thirty feet from their tent. Then he joined Emily as she stood at the edge of the small brook. She said, "You're going to take the sergeant's test, aren't you?" The words came out more as a statement than a question.

"Yes, I am."

"And you will come out number one on the list, right?"

"I will work hard to get as high on the list as I can."

"No, you will work to come out number one, and I'm going to help you study."

"Number one. That's my goal."

"I'm going to work on more balance in my life. Try to become more active, keep healthy. Try to keep up with you."

Gerald put his arm around Emily and gently squeezed her close and said, "You're healthy and smart and beautiful, and you're on the way to becoming a great attorney. And I think I'm the one who has to keep up with you."

Emily returned his squeeze and drew a deep breath through her nose. After a long exhale, she said, "I think we somehow balance each other out."

7

Saturday
July 8
2300 hours

SERGEANT MITCH REILLY LOADED UP his cruiser with his briefcase full of forms, a couple of novels, the afternoon paper, clipboard, ticket books, dictionary, power bars, nightstick, reference books for Connecticut General Statutes, pens, pencils, spare reading glasses, and a water bottle. The only thing he needed now to get him through this overtime midnight shift was a tall cup of coffee. As he closed the cruiser door, he caught sight of the vice-intelligence-narcotics guys leaving to go home. Reilly's mood began to sour. He had been a detective in VINs for years. When he made sergeant, he was transferred out of VINs and into patrol for a while. Then it was back into the detective bureau as a supervisor. His career path had always been a step forward and up, despite being outspoken against policies of the administration. That changed years ago.

Reilly had a habit of speaking his mind first and thinking about it later, and a decade ago, this got him transferred out of the bureau and onto midnight patrol over the course of two days. Midnights were where they sent you for punishment if they—the chiefs—didn't have enough for an official disciplinary action, but you'd pissed them off. And Reilly had *really* pissed off his chief in one little newspaper interview.

Now, for the umpteenth time, Reilly ran the events through

his head. The chief of police had sat there in a town hall meeting and point-blank told the town council and citizens that there were no drugs in town and no gang members. A reporter for the paper had recorded the meeting for the local news column. After working as an undercover officer and participating in over sixty undercover drug buys, over two hundred drug raids, and working dozens of snitches, Reilly knew there was and always would be drugs in town. He took the chief's statement as a slap in the face of the hard and dangerous work he and other officers had done.

But Reilly thought the biggest kick to the balls was the lack of integrity the chief had displayed when he made those statements. He was always harping on integrity, but here he was telling the council and citizens an outright lie, and they, in the warm fog of ignorant bliss, had bought into it. Reilly had decided he was going to set things right and met with a reporter. A week later, an article came out stating there were drugs in town and a gang problem, naming Reilly as the source. The article had mentioned where a recognized gang symbol had been carved into the sidewalk in front of the police station, inscribed there by gang members a month earlier when the cement was still wet during repairs.

The chief had wanted to fire Reilly, but after scrutinizing the town employment rules, he discovered he couldn't. As one union advocate pointed out, just because Reilly was a police officer, it didn't remove his right to free speech, especially in this case where his objective appeared to be genuinely informing the general public of a real threat. Rumor was that the chief had snapped, and Reilly wished he had been a fly on the wall to watch the fireworks. Once the dust settled, Reilly had been reassigned to midnight patrol. The workload was easy, but the hours sucked the life out of you. He quietly worked mids, looking forward to a few months down the road when he could put in a bid to be reassigned, and his seniority would count toward a shift he wanted.

Looking back, Reilly recalled some advice he'd gotten from a lieutenant shortly after he was reassigned. "Don't forget the lengths this administration will go for retribution. You're high on their list, and the chief, quote, hates your guts, unquote."

Now Rcilly could count the weeks to his retirement. He held a large coffee in one hand as he slowly drove through the quiet town. *Well*, Reilly thought, *I'd rather have the chief hate my guts and keep my integrity than be one of the two-faced pricks that spend a portion of each day in the chief's office, spouting false stories about their colleagues for the sole purpose of getting ahead.* The image of Officer Prentiss Pearson walking into the chief's office floated into Reilly's head.

Reilly pulled into the high school parking lot, noticing an old red Mustang 5.0 behind him that continued north on Dolen Street. After a slow drive around the back of the school, Reilly parked by the old tennis courts and sipped his coffee while hc tried to decide between reading a book or a magazine.

The patrol radio came alive. "Units Thirty-Three, Thirty-Four, and Forty. Report of a car into a tree, 300 block of Dolen Street, with injuries." Each unit responded with a code-three response, lights and sirens on. The crash was only about a half-mile from where Reilly had been parked and when he pulled up, Unit Thirty-Four, Officer Pete Slisz, was already there, standing in the middle of the wreck, trying to find a pulse on one of the two boys, victims of speed and inexperience. Reilly parked his cruiser at an angle so the headlights would be on the scene, also pointed his spotlight onto the wreck, then began to process what he saw.

The red Mustang 5.0 he'd seen moments earlier was now wrapped around a thick oak tree in the neat front yard of a residence. The body of the vehicle was bent at more than a ninety-degree angle. Someone who stood on the side of the tree opposite of the impact would be able to touch the front fender and rear fender at the same time with each hand. The driver's side door had popped free, putting the interior of the car on full display. The center of the impact was on the passenger's side, directly into the door, and a teenage boy sat there, unresponsive, with his eyes closed and legs pinned. The impact had placed the boy almost on top of the driver—another teenage boy, who, like his passenger, was motionless.

"I didn't get a pulse on that one," Pete said to Reilly, referring to the driver. "I think I have a weak one on this boy."

"Expedite medical," Reilly said into his shoulder mic. "Two casualties unresponsive, not breathing."

"Medics en route," came back dispatch. *Not fast enough,* thought Reilly as he futilely tried to find a pulse on the driver.

"What do you want me to do?" asked Officer Andy Peppers, the district officer who would handle the initial documentation of this crash.

"Run the plate, and I'll try to find out who these kids are, see if I can find a wallet with ID on them," Reilly replied, feeling through the pockets of the driver.

"I know these kids," said Pete. "They're going to be seniors in the high school—good kids." Reilly glanced at Pete, recalling he was the full-time school resource officer, currently putting in some patrol overtime on the midnight shift.

"Sorry, Pete." Not knowing what else to say, Reilly asked if there was still a pulse.

"I think so, very weak," Pete responded.

Reilly found a wallet in the left hip pocket of one of the young driver's jeans and pulled it out. Like most teenagers, there wasn't much in it—a high school ID card and a driver's license. Reilly handed the license to Andy and asked, "You know the registered owner of the car yet?"

"Waiting for a reply."

"Okay, you'll handle the initial case, and I'll call in the accident reconstruction team to do their thing."

"No problem."

"Either of them going to make it?"

"Doesn't look like it."

It only took three minutes for the paramedics and fire department to arrive and descend on the scene. Reilly would later reflect that when you felt helpless or overwhelmed, time stood still while you waited for help.

Reilly stood at the curb, taking in the scene again. His eyes fell to the boys, exposed and suspended in the open wreck. Pete had been talking to each of them in a quiet, reassuring voice, and was now walking away from the wreck toward Reilly with his head bowed as the paramedics took over the scene.

Reilly noticed a small group of teenagers standing near a cruiser that was blocking the road and nodded to Pete.

"I'll go talk to them," Pete said.

Reilly nodded, "Maybe we can find out where these boys were coming from. See if we can find out what led to this." Pete walked slowly away toward the small group of kids.

Reilly sat back in his cruiser and went through his mental checklist of things to do at fatal crash scenes; everything that needed to be done was happening, so for the moment, he was a spectator. Reilly watched the paramedics remove the driver's body from the wreck. They placed him on the grass about twenty feet away, pulling a yellow plastic blanket over him, then hurried back to the wreck. It was obvious they were having a more difficult time freeing the passenger, urgently working to give emergency medical care to the boy as they tried to extricate him. The boy under the yellow blanket was now a lifeless body, not in any need of urgency. He no longer had any needs.

Unable to sit still, Reilly approached a fire lieutenant and waited for him to finish talking on his radio, then asked, "What's it look like for the kid still in the car?"

"He's still alive, but it doesn't look good," the fire lieutenant said. "There was no sign of life on the first one, so we had to move him out of the way quickly to get to the second. You know who he is?"

"We found a license on the driver. His name is Steve Blake, lives a few blocks from here. We'll make notifications in a little while. Which hospital is the passenger going to go once you extricate him?"

"We're sending him to Hartford Hospital."

Reilly nodded and turned back to his cruiser. Pete met him in the middle of the road. "Hey, Sarge, the couple over there, walking up the sidewalk—they're the parents of one of the kids. Word got out pretty quickly about the accident. I guess there was a gathering at a kid's house. Supposedly no alcohol or drugs, and the kids I talked to appeared straight. These two in the Mustang left about a half-hour ago." Pete motioned toward the wreck. "Some of the other kids were driving home when they saw us and all the activity. They recognized the red fenders and white stripes of the car and started making phone calls and texting. Want me to handle the parents?"

"No, I got it. Just tell them to stand by my cruiser for a few minutes. I'll grab the kid's license from Andy. Remove any confusion, you know."

"Thanks, Sarge. I really didn't want to tell them."

"You've already done plenty tonight, Pete. If I could ask you to do one more thing, just get the names of the kids who were at the gathering. We'll want to talk to them later."

Reilly retrieved the license from Andy and walked back to his cruiser, suddenly feeling the whole scene was surreal. The flashing emergency lights from nearly a dozen vehicles reflected off faces, houses, and vegetation. Loud generators were being fired up to power the spotlights that would illuminate the broken car and the broken body lying next to it, as if they were the lead act in a show.

Surreality was a feeling Reilly had felt many times as an

officer—the simultaneous effect of adrenaline and fear on the body. The numbness. The intense focus. Only through experience did a cop learn to control it and make it work for him. The more times one faced a situation causing fear and worked through it successfully, the less overwhelming future situations became. But there was one thing Reilly always had a hard time with—informing parents that their child was dead. *This is going to suck*, he thought, *but I'm the ranking officer here—my job.*

He approached the couple. "Good evening, I'm Sergeant Reilly. I understand you may be the parents of one of the boys in the car?" The man and woman, who each appeared to be in their mid-forties, were holding hands, their entire bodies trembling. Both weakly nodded. "What's the name of your son?" Reilly asked.

"Steven Blake," said the father. Reilly glanced at the driver's license he held in his hand.

"And where does he live?"

"With us on Margery Circle."

No doubt about it, thought Reilly as he looked at the address on the driver's license. *This is their son. Just tell them.*

He took a deep breath. "Unfortunately, I have bad news—the worst news, and there's no way to say it easily. Your son, Steven, is dead. He died in the crash."

Both parents started trembling more, almost uncontrollably now, shaking their heads *no*. "He's under the yellow blanket on the lawn across the street. If you would like, I can walk you over there. You can sit and be with him as long as you need."

"Why aren't they helping him?" the mother cried.

"There's nothing they can humanly do, ma'am. The paramedics here are the best. There's nothing that can be done." Reilly's mind scrambled for something else to say, to try to ease the pain, and he remembered an article he had read about a first responder who would inform family

71

members their loved ones had died quickly and without any pain or suffering. According to the article, that information had helped the families in their grief. Reilly started: "I was at the scene within a minute of the crash. Neither boy suffered any pain."

The mother exploded into sobs. The father, tears streaming down his cheeks, his head shaking *no*, forced out his only words: "I never should have bought him that Mustang."

Reilly quietly excused himself, letting the parents know how to contact him if they had any questions.

To Reilly and the other cops, these were two teenage boys driving too fast, and they'd paid a steep price for it. To the parents, these were their sons who only a few years ago were babies they held in their arms, kids playing Little League and soccer and opening Christmas presents. Reilly understood all of that. *So why would you buy your seventeen-year-old boy a Mustang 5.0?* Mixing teenage boys and fast cars always ended up a fucking mess. *That father will never be able to forgive himself,* thought Reilly as he glanced at the twisted wreck under the spotlights.

"You'll be front row to the greatest show on earth," is how one FTO explained what being a cop was like when Reilly was a rookie. Walking under the spotlights now, Reilly felt like the ringmaster. *Look to your left, ladies and gentlemen, a dead teenage boy! Center ring is the car he was driving, nicely wrapped around a tree! To the right is the ambulance speeding away to take the passenger, who will soon be declared dead, to the hospital. Exiting stage left are one boy's parents, their pain on display for all to see . . .*

Hours later, Reilly returned to the scene. The controlled chaos following the crash had long since been replaced with the steady, and somewhat dull, movements of the accident reconstruction team. In this case, two officers were armed with cameras, a measuring tape, a tripod device similar to what a surveyor would use, and large notepads. One of the officers called Reilly over.

"Hey, Sarge, check it out." Reilly followed him to a point in the road a hundred feet south of the tree that had stopped the Mustang. "You can see a skid mark start in the northbound lane, cross over the southbound, and hit this curb."

"Yeah, I see it," replied Reilly.

"Now, look toward the wreck."

"Okay . . ."

"This skid mark leads straight towards the wreck, but there's no marks in the grass. Get it? The Mustang hit this six-inch-high curb so hard and fast the curb sent it airborne, never touching the ground again, for one hundred feet before it hit that tree."

"Fuckin' A. What does that translate into for speed prior to impact?"

"I still have to calculate it. I'm guessing over one hundred miles per hour."

"Fuckin' A," Reilly repeated. "You going to the postmortem tomorrow?"

"Yeah."

"Let me know what the ME says actually killed them. I'm curious because neither boy had a mark on him. No blood, obvious broken bones, nothing."

"I'll keep you posted."

"Thanks."

At the end of his shift, Reilly walked into the watch commander's office at 0700 hours, holding the package of reports and a small press release regarding the fatal crash in a manila folder. Newly promoted Lieutenant Lilly Felders was talking on the phone to a citizen, and Reilly waited for her to finish before handing her the package.

"You say that your son is being recruited for a gang?" Lilly said into the phone. "Okay, well, the chief has said there are no gangs in town. . . . We don't have the resources to investigate that, ma'am. I can send an officer to take a report. . . . You don't want to make a report? Then we really can't help you." Lilly hung up, shrugged her shoulders, and looked at Reilly.

"There are no gangs in town, so we don't investigate gang activity, huh?" said Reilly.

"Just telling them what the chief says," replied Lilly.

"Chief's been saying that for years. Maybe we should get him to say there are no burglaries or robberies, too, and we won't have to investigate those crimes either."

"Yeah." Lilly beamed at the thought. "That would be great. Then we wouldn't have to do all this paperwork and bullshit."

Reilly realized Lilly would like that to happen, and once again concluded that it really *was* possible to promote a person beyond their capabilities. "Here's the package on the fatal last night. Hopefully, everything is in there, and I won't get a phone call during the day—which is actually when midnight shift people sleep—asking me a stupid question."

"I'll put it right here." Lilly turned and placed it on top of another stack of reports.

Ten minutes later, Reilly walked out of headquarters into the bright summer sunlight. The cool morning air was giving way to warmth and bright sunshine, lightening people's moods with the promise of a long and warm day. *One of the nicest days of the year is going to be the darkest and worst for two families,* Reilly mused as he climbed into his truck.

It's the stark contrast, light and dark, good and evil, courage and cowardice, stupidity and brilliance, humor and sullenness, that cops witness. Sometimes all in the same shift. Front row seat to the greatest show on earth. Reilly selected some mellow music from the Cowboy Junkies on his iPod, put his truck in drive, and headed home. *Fuckin' A.*

8

Wednesday
July 12
2144 hours

DONNA DROVE THE CRUISER THROUGH the light rain, unconsciously squinting as she labored to see through the streaked windshield. "These wipers aren't very good," she grumbled to Gerald.

"No, but they're about average for what you're going to get in a cruiser. For what it's worth, you can note it down on the car sheet and turn it into the mail slot for fleet maintenance. Try turning up the defroster."

"If I do that, the heat will be blown back into my eyes and dry out my contacts."

Gerald shrugged. "Some guys pack Rain Away in their duty bag. When it rains, they'll find an overhang, like a bank drive-through, and apply it to the windshield before the start of their shift. It definitely helps."

"Good idea, but it's not going to help me now."

"I might have some in my personal vehicle. If you want to head back to headquarters, I can check."

Before Donna could change direction, they caught a call. "Units Twenty-Two and Twenty-Five, some kind of disturbance behind the Baker's Pride Bakery, Two-Nineteen Main Street. Could be people dumpster diving. . . . The bakery owner is very upset and hard to understand," came the dispatch.

"We're close to Baker's Pride," Gerald said. "We'll worry about the windshield later." Gerald and Donna were assigned as the backup unit and arrived at the same time as the primary unit, Unit Twenty-Two, otherwise known as twenty-year veteran Officer Dick Demao. As the two cruisers pulled into the ten-space rear parking lot, their headlights shone on one skinny white male, shirtless, his dark hair a wet mullet, hands jammed into his jean pockets, standing alone. His pale white skin was shiny from the drizzle. He was staring in the direction of another white male a few feet away, facedown on his knees, not quite into the narrow space between a dumpster and stained brick wall of the bakery. Demao followed mullet's gaze, clicking on his spotlight and focusing it on the base of the dumpster. The body there was slumped forward, face turned sideways and flush against the wet pavement with his bare ass in the air. The poor fellow's pants and underwear were down to his knees. Demao got out of his cruiser and glanced at mullet, then bare-ass. His shoulders slumped in resignation as his mind assessed what his eyes were seeing. Slamming his car door shut, he walked over to bare-ass.

"Just observe what's going on and note down any questions you may have, and we'll review this incident later," Gerald said to Donna as they walked from their cruiser and sidled up to the wet mullet male. Gerald asked in a most non-confrontational way: "So . . . what's going on?"

"I don't know—I was just sleeping, and all of a sudden, you guys were here," the male responded.

"What's your name?"

"David."

"Okay, David, why don't you have a seat in the back of my car to stay dry, while I try to figure out why we were called here."

Once David was secured in the back of Gerald's cruiser, Gerald walked over to Demao, who was standing over the body of the bare-assed, facedown, fetal-positioned male. Demao wasn't smiling. "This is your beat, isn't it?" he asked.

"Nope," Gerald said with a smile, "mine ends one block over. This one's yours. Why?"

"This guy's dead," Demao replied.

Gerald bent down, looking closer at the body. Lividity had set in. He had been dead for at least a couple of hours. "Yup, you're right. He's dead," Gerald deadpanned.

"And it looks like he got ass-fucked," Demao exclaimed. "I mean, how do I write this one up? 'His asshole looked rose-colored as if unlubricated friction had been applied to it.' I don't know what an asshole that's just been fucked looks like."

"I'm happy to say, neither do I," replied Gerald.

By now, the street sergeant, Sergeant Onslow, had arrived and walked close enough to hear the last bit of the two street cops' conversation. "This is *his* beat, isn't it, Sarge?" Demao said.

The sergeant looked around. "I don't think so, but this is what we'll do. Gerald, you go interview the guy in the back of your cruiser, and Demao and I will talk to the folks in the bakery. The medics will be here in a minute to make the presumption of death notice, so let's get one of your cameras out and snap some photos before they come and contaminate the scene."

Gerald took a set of pictures, an overall picture, then a near shot of the dead body, and then several close-ups with a running commentary to Donna on why each picture is important. Gerald gave Donna a quick lesson on lividity, the pooling of blood under the skin of a deceased body, and estimation of time of death ending with the statement, "This guy's OFD."

"OFD?" asked Donna.

"Obviously fucking dead," said Gerald.

"I'm going to chat this guy David up. How about if you stand outside the cruiser and listen? I'll keep the windows open, but I want to be one on one with David while I talk to him." Donna nodded in agreement while Gerald got back into his cruiser and started talking. "So, David, I just need to know how you know that guy behind the dumpster, um— what's his name, anyway?"

"I know him as Brian. Just met him earlier today," David replied slowly, unsure of what else the cop might ask.

"So tell me about you and Brian."

Gerald listened as David, through his heroin-and alcohol-addled mind, told his story, much to Gerald's amusement. *Good times,* thought Gerald as he wrote his notes. When David finished, Gerald politely excused himself, exited the cruiser, and headed over to Demao and Onslow. Donna trailed behind, curious as to how the veteran officers would react to David's story.

"Here's what I got," Gerald started. "According to David, he met Brian earlier this afternoon, and they started sharing a forty of beer. Both were probably already intoxicated before they met. So they finish the forty and Brian starts feeling up David, who doesn't like it, but Brian was apparently a persistent kind of homo, and David gives in to Brian's charms. They have sex behind the dumpster. Shortly after that, Brian takes a nap, 'cause like any of us, once you blow a nut, you either take a nap or make a sandwich." The two male cops hearing the story unconsciously nodded in agreement. "Brian goes to sleep, and David goes on the search for some more cheap alcohol. While he's away drinking, he gets horny again and figures it's easier to go back to Brian than pick up one of the local sluts—he figures a piece of ass is a piece of ass. David finds Brian still asleep and, thinking with his dick, rolls Brian into his current ass-fuck position and starts cornholing him when someone from the bakery came out. Then we showed up."

"So David fucked a dead guy up the ass is what we got," said Onslow, smiling.

"Which is sex assault four," chimed in Gerald.

"What do you mean?" said Demao.

"Brian, being dead, couldn't give consent. So David is charged with sex four."

Demao looked at Onslow, who was nodding in agreement and clarified, "It's actually written right there in the third sentence of the statute for sex assault four, no sex with a dead person. It's only a misdemeanor, so David isn't too screwed. But he does go to jail tonight."

"Fucking wonderful," muttered Demao, knowing he'd have to fill out all of the paperwork for the case, which would likely take the rest of the shift.

"Can you get him to sign a statement with that story, Gerald?" the sergeant said.

"Yeah, I can. He thinks I'm his friend."

"Does he know he just fucked a dead guy in the ass?"

"No, he thinks Brian is just passed out, and we're waiting for him to wake up and make sure he's okay."

It was close to midnight when Gerald and Donna started to review her Daily Observation Report, DOR, while parked in the corner of a commuter lot. "Any thoughts on our two lovers earlier tonight?" Gerald asked.

"It's a whole other world that I'm seeing for the first time, and I like venturing out into it," Donna answered.

Gerald grunted an "uh-huh" and continued checking off boxes on the DOR.

Donna continued, "Part of me thinks it's sad, you know, the way the two guys behind the dumpster live. Part of me thinks it's pretty funny, especially the way you guys handled it. But I guess the biggest thing I feel is the desire to see more and be a part of what's going on out here on the street. I want to make things right."

Gerald handed the DOR to Donna for her review and signature then said, "Police work is entertaining, and the bizarre stuff is what we get to see. It really is why a lot of us come to work each day. It also helps to have a weird sense of humor. As far as making things right, well, you're not going to make everything right. If you can make a few things okay for the moments that you are involved, then you're doing pretty good."

Donna finished the conversation in her mind: *I'm going to make things right.*

David opened his eyes to the sound of the dayshift desk sergeant yelling through the bars of the cell. "Wake up, David—breakfast time." The sergeant placed a tray holding a lukewarm sausage and egg sandwich and a small cup of black coffee from McDonald's on the flat horizontal bar of the cell door.

"What am I here for?" David asked.

"You fucked a dead guy up the ass," replied the sergeant, who looked at David's eyes and thought, *It's like looking into the eyes of a cocker spaniel.*

9

Thursday
July 20
0050 hours

MITCH REILLY PARKED HIS TRUCK in his driveway, hit the garage door opener remote, and walked into his house through the garage, passing the row of neatly hanging fishing poles arranged in order by length on the pegboard wall of the garage. He didn't look at the tackle box on his workbench. It was in disarray and a bit depressing to look at. With all the overtime he was sucking up, he hadn't had time to organize it, never mind go fishing.

Mitch had just finished his regular second shift as patrol sergeant of C squad. He liked the officers assigned to the shift, but his boss, Lieutenant Cantu, was a slothful enigma who could never be found during a shift. Given this environment, Mitch pretty much ran the squad as he saw fit, and he drew satisfaction from knowing his band of officers had fewer citizen complaints and more arrests made than any other squad.

The shift had been slow, with few calls for service from the citizenry and few traffic stops or self-initiated investigations by the patrol officers. This kept Mitch's supervisory duties light and allowed him time, once again, to calculate his retirement package from the town. If the overtime, which is calculated into the formula for his final pension, kept steady, Mitch would be able to retire at the end of his twenty-fifth year, just weeks away, not having to stick around longer or going to work full time anywhere else. Many of his co-workers were not so fortunate. Some stayed on the job to keep family members with disabilities on the department's health insurance rolls. Some others were very fertile, starting second or even third families with their latest love interest, then working forever to support all the offspring and ex-spouses.

Grabbing a beer out of his fridge, he sat down on his living room couch, reclined, and pointed the remote at his TV. Mitch grumbled about fucking progressives as he channel-surfed past the usual late-night talk shows and their liberal commentary and humor.

He found The Real-Life Drama Channel documenting a Boston emergency room, following three patients from their arrival in the ER to discharge. *I don't usually watch this shit,* Mitch thought to himself, *but fuck it, nothing else is on.* Mitch clicked "OK" on the remote and reclined further. The first drama was a premature birth, the camera work was up close to show the anxiety and fear on family members' faces as they arrived. The producers then cut to the second drama, a car accident victim with serious injuries arriving in an ambulance. The camera was a step away from the EMS attendants, nurses, and doctors as they moved in an almost choreographed manner around the accident victim. An obvious head injury. Blood drips from the patient's ear, and he doesn't appear conscious. Quick and direct questions and answers between doctors, nurses, and EMTs before the doctors started giving orders. Mitch had seen all of this before in person and up close. It was entertainment for those in the world who lead dull lives or at least have dull livelihoods. The show's producers weren't playing up the drama; it was all there and didn't need any hyperbole. The third drama starts with the cameras on the faces of the ER personnel as a message is repeated over the PA system in the background, "Ambulance is two minutes out with a gunshot victim, a police officer, two minutes, gunshot victim, police officer." Mitch's skin went cold, and he unconsciously held his breath. The show cut to a commercial.

Mitch let out a long breath and took a sip from his still-full beer during the prolonged commercial break. *Shit still gets to me,* he thought silently, *but I'm good now.* The drama show starts again, ambulance doors swing open, and the cop gunshot victim is quickly wheeled out into the ER. Mitch starts to cry. *It's only a show, I'm not there, shit, why am I crying!* The EMS attendants talk to the victim, the cop, and he talks back to them. Nurses and doctors surround the gurney, and through the eye of the cameras, you can see that the cop is bare-chested and seems to be moving his arms on his own. The show goes back to the first patient, the premature birth then rotates through the stories of the three ER patients. Each rotation of the stories goes a little further into each drama. Each time the wounded cop drama came on, Mitch cried, but it was the only one of the dramas that produced tears. No emotions stirred in him watching the baby's birth or car accident victim.

The show ends on a positive note. All the ER patients in the show are going to survive. The cop had been shot in the chest but was wearing body armor. He was hurting from bruised muscle tissue and ribs. He would heal and be able to go back to work.

Mitch went into the kitchen and poured the last of his beer into the sink and wondered, *Is there something wrong with me? Why was I crying? . . . Jesus.* He quietly ascended the stairs and peeked into the two bedrooms where his son and daughter used to sleep. Both children had grown and were out of the house now, but Mitch relied on old habits. His older child, Teddy, was now a lieutenant in the Army, ROTC having paid for most of his college tuition. The younger child, Beth, was "free-spirited," in her mother's words. Mitch called her out of control. She was in California. Beth called her mother daily but rarely talked to Mitch.

Turning, he went into his bedroom and suddenly felt not just tired but weary as well. Sliding into bed, he pulled himself close to his wife and felt the warmth of her skin against his. She let out a soft moan but didn't move. Mitch closed his eyes and forced his face into the pillow. *There's nothing wrong with me, and even if there is, I can't say anything to anyone anyways. Fuck it.*

10

Friday
July 21
2200 hours

DONNA LOOKED AROUND THE LINEUP room. There were enough seats to handle up to twenty officers, but there were only five, besides her, in the room. No one talked to her; it would be her first time on the midnight shift. She sat in silence as a young sergeant holding a clipboard and squad assignment sheet walked into the room, gave a cursory glance at the officers in attendance and sat down. Donna did not know the sergeant, and it dawned on her that in this 24/7 job, there were a lot of co-workers she simply didn't know because they worked the opposite side of her schedule.

"As you can see, we are below our minimum staffing of eight officers for tonight, so we will have three on overtime joining us a little later," the sergeant stated. "Also, we have a new recruit with us, Donna Harris. Donna has to complete a couple of weeks with us on midnights before she can be cut loose from her FTO and work on her own."

Several of the officers, all men, turned their heads to look at Donna, but no one said anything. A moment passed, and they turned their attention back to the sergeant, who was picking a sticky note off of the squad assignment sheet. "Gerald is running late," the sergeant said as he crumpled the sticky note and threw it toward a wastebasket without looking and missed.

The sergeant scrutinized the notes on a clipboard with blue sheets of paper, the daily log, that he had brought in with him. He read the latest entry out loud: "The south end of town, mostly District Thirty-Five, is getting hit by people breaking into unlocked vehicles and stealing items from them. Citizens are coming out in the morning to find items such as loose change, cell phones, a purse from one vehicle, a laptop from another, were stolen out of the vehicles during the night. No suspects at this time."

The sergeant put down the clipboard and looked up. "As we all know, the suspects could be neighborhood kids getting their jollies stealing, or there's a junkie in the neighborhood supporting his habit or the delinquents from Hartford are trolling our town looking for easy targets. Any way you cut it, you should be checking on anyone out late to see if they have witnessed anything or are our suspects." The sergeant pulled a pencil from behind his ear, slid the squad assignment sheet in front of him, and, without looking up, said: "Pick your districts."

Gerald arrived at headquarters an hour later, cashing in an hour of comp time he had earned a month earlier, suited up, and met Donna outside the watch commander's office. "Cruiser all set to go?" Gerald asked Donna.

"All set," she replied, "we were assigned District Twenty-Five."

"Good. Let's go. I need a large coffee."

At the intersection of Main and Wells, Donna got back into their cruiser with two hot coffees. Gerald told her to start checking their beat, and she knew that meant to check on the all-night convenience stores at odd intervals and occasionally drive by the two bars in their beat that would be open for another hour. After a couple of sips of coffee

Gerald finally said, "I worked day shift overtime today, and after I got home, I couldn't fall asleep. Of course, I finally did two hours before I had to be back here. By the time I woke up, I knew I would be late, so that's why I came in a little late and a little groggy."

Donna just nodded her head as she drove. Gerald continued after another sip of coffee, "This shift can be exceedingly boring, but once in a while, we might get some good calls."

"Some good times?" Donna asked.

"Yeah, some good times," Gerald replied with a slight smile.

"District Twenty-Five, take a domestic at 22 Sanders Lane. Sounds verbal. Husband and wife, no weapons," came the disinterested voice over the cruiser radio.

Donna replied with a, "Roger," and they soon were on Sanders Lane, a dead-end street settled with small ranch and Cape-style homes. She parked two houses down from where the domestic was taking place.

"We get calls here every so often," Gerald said to Donna before they exited their cruiser. "The guy had a serious head injury from a construction accident a while back and sometimes goes off his rocker, and the wife has a hard time handling it. To my knowledge, they've never been physically violent to each other."

The two officers quietly exited their cruiser and walked across the small lawn toward the open front door, the storm door still closed. About ten feet from the door, with Gerald leading Donna, Gerald stopped and turned, putting his finger to his lips. They stood in silence in the dark, listening to the argument inside. Besides the yelling, and the extra noise of a small dog incessantly barking, there was no indication of physical violence. While they had been listening, one other officer, their backup, had silently walked up behind them.

Gerald looked behind him, and after a half-minute of listening to the dispute, he nodded his head, leaned in, and almost whispered into Donnas' ear, "You're the lead officer on this one."

Donna nodded and climbed the front stoop while Gerald and the backup stood a few steps away on the lawn. Donna eased the storm door open just a few inches and shouted into the house, "Police. Can you come to the front door?"

A male voice from inside yelled, "You called the cops? Jesus fucking Christ! Let yourselves in! I don't give a fuck!"

Donna peered cautiously around the doorjamb first, then fully opened the door and walked in with Gerald following. A small dog, still yip-barking, ran past them out the door.

Donna and Gerald took a few steps into the small house, which placed them at the edge of the living room. There, sitting, sunk into the deep cushions of the couch, was a skinny male who appeared to be in his mid-forties, his skin as white as notepaper that contrasted with his black chest hair, leg hair, and crotch hair sticking out from under his yellow thong. Standing in the room at the far end of the couch was a woman, about the same age, who appeared to be only wearing a dirty T-shirt that barely came down to her thighs. Looking at her, the word "frumpy" came to Donna's mind.

"I ain't talkin' to any of you," the couch-sitting male stated as his eyes darted back and forth between Donna and Gerald.

"How about you just give me your name?" Donna countered but got no reply. Donna turned to the frumpy woman and said, "Can I talk to you in the hallway?" Frumpy answered with a slight nod.

As Donna walked into the short hallway, Gerald centered himself in the middle of the living room and started talking to the male whom he knew from past encounters by his first name. "Hey, John. What the hell, buddy? We can hear you guys all the way down the street. It's the middle of the night, and you guys are making all this noise. Tell me what's going on, man."

"Fuck it," John said as he sulked, eyes staring at the floor. "I don't want to say anything."

Gerald persisted, "Dude, you're sitting there in your yellow-banana-hammock-guy-thong with two cops in your living room at midnight. C'mon, tell me what the problem is."

John was silent for a few seconds then abruptly looked Gerald in the eye, pointed in the direction of Frumpy, and blurted out, "She wants me to eat her pussy, and I don't want to eat her pussy. Look at her. She's fat. Her underwear has piss and shit stains on them, and she hasn't taken a bath in days. I don't want to eat her pussy! Would you eat her pussy! Would you? Fuck if I am!"

Donna heard their backup officer by the front door snort as he stifled a laugh and excused himself, saying something about going to look for the dog. The frumpy woman stood in front of Donna as Donna pursed her lips to keep from smiling. She heard Gerald, "See John, that wasn't so bad. Now we can talk to her to see if we can impart a little advice on personal hygiene, and we'll be out of here." John let out a snort as Gerald continued. "John, what's your last name again and date of birth?"

Donna opened her mouth to talk to the frumpy woman, but no words came out. After an awkward pause, words Gerald had constantly preached to her finally came to her mind: *Just start a normal conversation with some easy questions.* Finally, Donna asked the woman her name and date of birth, was she injured—the questions cops always ask. The woman said her name was Mary, born in June 1975, and she wasn't injured. Donna was taking her time making her notes when Gerald walked up behind Mary. Gerald said in a low voice, "So . . . Mary. John said nothing physical happened here tonight. Is that right?"

Mary turned, trying to talk politely to both officers now on either side of her. "He just started yelling about . . . what he told you about," Mary said.

"Do you feel threatened by him in any way? Do you feel safe staying here?" Gerald asked.

"I feel safe. I didn't think he needed to yell at me."

"As a police officer, I don't usually give out advice on couples and their sex lives, Mary, but personally, my wife and I always shower before we have sex." Mary nodded, and then Gerald said, "You guys are a nice couple, and you both are working through some tough problems. Keep trying your best, and I think things will work out for you guys." Gerald glanced at Donna and leaned his head toward the front door.

Picking up the cue, Donna said, "We're gonna go now and see if we can find your dog. If you think things are getting out of control again, call us back."

Ten minutes later, Donna and Gerald were in their cruiser, still parked two houses down from John and Mary's house. It was Gerald's suggestion to sit and write the report while they were still there in case John started yelling at Mary again.

"Sorry, I kinda took over that case," Gerald said to Donna.

Donna replied, "Normally, I would be a little ticked that you jumped in, but I was working hard not to laugh, you know, keep my composure."

"Yeah, it can be tough sometimes, but these two, they are never violent towards each other. They just have low coping skills to begin with, and since John had his head injury, he snaps and yells at her, and she can't deal with it. They probably don't get much positive reassurance in their lives, so the little pep talk at the end there hopefully helps. But Jesus, seriously, wash your fucking pussy. For once, I don't blame the guy."

Donna absently nodded her head in agreement as she tapped the keys on the MDT.

The remainder of the midnight shift remained quiet, just a few false alarms from some commercial buildings that required Gerald and Donna to walk the perimeter of the structures and check for open doors or windows. If they found none, they filled out an alarm form, placing one copy of the form on the front door of the business and one copy on the watch commander's desk at the end of the shift.

"Literally one or two out of a thousand alarms are real," Gerald had said while he was filling out her DOR at the end of their shift, "but you have to check each one like it's an active burglary because you never know when those one or two are coming."

Donna nodded her head in agreement and said, "That seems rather obvious."

"Yes, it is obvious, but human nature can take over, and cops get lazy going to so many false alarms. That's when bad shit happens." Gerald turned to Donna and said, "Don't get lazy."

Usually, because Gerald had to fill out the DOR and expose Donna to as much patrol work as possible, such as fielding calls other officers were loath to respond to near the end of a shift, they were the last officers to walk in the back door of headquarters and run "the gauntlet" to turn in their cruiser keys and paperwork.

The back door was where patrol officers congregated to wait out the last few minutes of their shift while the oncoming shift prepared for their day. Standing on the short staircase, leaning against walls on each side, they formed a short, two-panel roasting party that the late arrivals of a given shift had to pass through on their way in. These end-of-shift gatherings at the back door, known as the gauntlet, had become the de facto location where rumors were started, expanded, debunked, or glorified for the sole purpose of amusement. To pass through was an invitation for any past mistake to come to light. One officer, who years earlier had lost a fight with a feral cat he had been trying to humanely catch, resulting in the shredding of his uniform pant legs as well as his skin, was still greeted with meows and hisses whenever he had to walk the gauntlet. The cat was never captured. Faux "wanted" posters with cute kittens depicted as the suspect were pasted to the officer's locker. Whenever he would take them down, more would show up. Eventually, the officer stopped ripping them down, and they became the permanent décor of his locker. It was just one example where deprecating humor and peer pressure did more to self-discipline a squad of officers than a volume of general orders.

The story of John and Mary's sexual hygiene had made the rounds thanks to the backup officer who repeated the story to the entire squad. Gerald knew something was up when he opened the back door and observed a half-dozen smiling faces gazing back at him. He started up the stairs with Donna a step behind when one of the midnight guys, Officer Poulson, opened up, "So Donna, what do you wash before you sleep with someone?"

Donna stopped, looked into the eyes of her agitator, and said, "My hoo ha."

"What's a hoo ha?"

"It's what's between your legs. The only question I have for you is: Is it bald like your head?"

The stairwell erupted in laughter as snaps and verbal barbs fell on the officer. Gerald and Donna continued on to the watch commander's office. "Nice comeback," Gerald said.

"I'm kind of surprised I said it," Donna replied. "I usually don't make fun of people, but I'm tired, and I guess I have less of a filter to what I say. I feel a little bad about making fun of his bald head."

"Don't feel bad. He started it, and you finished it. But now you do have to go back to the gauntlet and hang out. If you don't, then they'll think you're hiding and afraid to come back."

"So, let's go."

Gerald and Donna sidled back to the top of the stairwell, where the officers were talking about having a few beers at the Last Precinct. One of the officers, Lenny, turned to

Gerald and Donna and said, "You guys want to join us for a beer or two?"

"Sure," Gerald said. Donna was cautious, not sure if drinking alcohol, even off duty, was a smart thing to do while still on FTO.

She responded, "I'd like to, but I'm not a member."

"You don't have to be," said Lenny, "as long as you sign in as a guest, it's all legit."

Donna looked at Gerald, whose noncommittal shrug of his shoulders showed it wasn't his decision to make. "Sure, I'll come," Donna answered.

Inside the woman's locker room, Donna changed into leggings and what she called a butt-covering sweatshirt. Untying her ponytail, she quickly massaged her scalp, letting her shoulder-length hair fall naturally. Her eyes were dry, and she replaced her irritating contact lenses with dark-rimmed glasses. Placing a University of Maine Black Bears hockey hat on her head, she went out to her car, a five-year-old silver Hyundai.

Pulling up to the Last Precinct, Donna found a side door propped open by a rolled-up newspaper. She stepped inside and stopped momentarily to allow for her eyes to adjust to the dim interior. Lenny called from behind the bar to remind her to sign the register by the door, which she did while noting the stale cigarette smoke in the air. *I'm going to have to wash these clothes when I get home,* she thought. Stepping up to the bar, she noticed that three of her male squadmates already in attendance were appraising her with elevator eyes, and she wondered how her attire of leggings under a baggy sweatshirt ranked in their minds. *This is a male-dominated profession,* one of her female academy instructors had cautioned during one class, *be mindful of how you interact with your colleagues, especially when you are new.*

Donna ordered a Bud Light and sat on one of the vinyl-covered bar stools. She broke out a twenty to pay for the beer, but Lenny waved it away. "I got the first round," he said.

Donna placed the twenty on the bar top and said, "I'll get the second round."

Lenny nodded approvingly and placed small wood coins in front of the others at the bar. "Coming up the gauntlet, you had a great comeback for Poulson. He thought you were an easy target." Lenny said.

"I normally don't like to pick on people, but he caught me off guard, and I snapped back at him," Donna looked around, "Is he here, in the backroom or something?"

"No, he isn't going to come here now. He's afraid of getting his balls busted even more after you put him in his place."

"Now I do feel bad. . . ."

"Don't. He had it coming after his comment to you. We're all big boys and girls here. If you can't take it, keep your mouth shut."

Donna took a small sip from her beer, nodding her head slightly.

Gerald came in and sat at the opposite end of the bar from Donna. Lenny had a Budweiser open for him before his ass hit the seat. "So, Gerald, how's our new rookie coming along?" Lenny asked.

"You know I can't comment on a new officer's performance," Gerald replied. "But I can say this—she makes few mistakes and never the same mistake twice."

"Good to hear. Any problem keeping yourselves busy last night? It was pretty slow."

"It was pretty slow, but I'm studying for the sergeant's test, so when we run out of patrol activities, I break out the general orders book and make notes for myself."

"What does Donna do while you're studying?"

"She drives around looking for criminal activity or citizens in need of help."

Lenny smiled at the well-worn answer most officers gave

when asked by a supervisor of what their patrol activities of the shift had been.

The two squadmates seated between Donna and Gerald had kept to themselves, not having glanced at Donna since their initial gaze when she walked in and not getting involved in any conversation. Donna noticed there were three empty beers in front of each of them, and they already cashed in their wooden nickels for the round she was buying. One of the two turned to Gerald and said, "By my count, you would make about fourteen guys taking the sergeant's test."

"Sounds about right," Gerald replied.

"Good luck with it. From where I stand, there's about three ass-kissers taking the exam that you'll have to beat. Even if you do finish at the top, the admin will skip over you to promote one of their ass-kissers."

"Rule of three, I know it," Gerald said and then recited the rule: "At the chief's discretion, he can skip up to two candidates on the promotion list to promote the third."

"Theoretically, the guys who place third, sixth, and ninth could get promoted one, two, three. In fact, ten years ago, I saw a guy who had placed sixth get promoted over four guys who were ahead of him on the list."

"I've heard the story. It comes up every time there's a promotional exam."

"It's not a story. I was one of the guys who was skipped on the list. Came in second out of nineteen who took the test. Three failed the test outright. The chiefs wanted number six and seven on the list, they were true suck-dick-ass-kissers. Even though I was skipped, I was still eligible, and I had some people tell me that I would get promoted, almost promised me, but it never happened. The admin kept the list active until they could advance number seven. The next day they terminated the list. Anybody on the list, regardless of ranking, would have to take the test over the next time it was posted. I said fuck it and never tried again."

"Well, Marty, I'll just have to take my chances," Gerald deadpanned.

Marty took a last pull from his beer and said, "Good luck to ya, Gerry, you would make a fine sergeant." Marty pushed himself away from the bar and walked out the door. As soon as the door closed behind him, Lenny glanced at Donna and said what was obvious to everyone who worked with Marty for a period of time. "He's very bright and an excellent cop, but he is also a world-class ball-buster and rumor-starter. No chief will knowingly promote those traits into the supervisory ranks."

Donna smiled as she looked at Gerald and said, "I thought you didn't like people calling you Gerry?"

"I don't. That's Lenny's point. Marty busts balls whenever he can, even to people he likes."

Lenny turned to Donna and asked, "I have a woman fashion question for you. . . . A for-real question."

"Okay."

"Why do fat women wear ripped jeans? I mean that as an honest question. I want to hear it from a woman's point of view."

"I don't know. Maybe they just want to keep up with the latest fashion."

"But it makes it look like the cellulite in their fat legs is bursting through their jeans. It's not really all that attractive."

"You mean like when a fat hairy guy wears a tank top, looking like a worn Brillo pad with tits?" said Donna.

Lenny furrowed his brow for a moment, "I see what you're saying, and it ain't pretty."

Donna and Lenny clinked their bottles to celebrate their mutual understanding of fashion.

Finishing her beer, Donna excused herself, telling Lenny and Gerald the two beers were having more of an effect on her after being up all night.

Her commute usually took twenty to thirty minutes during the day, but this Sunday morning, with little to no traffic, she was home to her apartment in fifteen minutes. She thought about her co-workers during the drive. She felt they were all cut from the same cloth, willing to take risks to defend the citizens of their town, and all would defend each other in any circumstance. She took a warm comfort in being accepted, so far, by her fellow law enforcement officers. She knew she still had to prove herself, but at the moment, she felt content. She couldn't be happier with her job or the people she worked with. Ten minutes after she had parked her Hyundai, she was in a deep slumber.

11

Saturday
July 22
0930 hours

GERALD SAT AT HIS KITCHEN table and spread the six books out in front of him. Up until now, his studying had been haphazard, and Emily had noticed. A few days earlier, she had picked up the study guidebook and noticed the self-test questions at the end of a chapter and began peppering him with those queries at different times of the day. It irritated him that Emily had jumped into what he considered his business, but he was more irritated with himself for the half-assed answers he had given. Time to focus and get organized.

The six books were from the recommended reading list for the upcoming sergeant's exam. One was *Criminal Investigations*, a thick tome detailing investigative procedures for sexual assaults, homicides, burglaries, and almost any other crime ever committed. The authors walked the reader through every detail of almost any kind of investigation. Over four hundred pages' worth of investigative particulars and minutiae. Another publication on his table, *Modern Community Policing, How to Garner Respect From Your Community*, was authored by a couple of professors of social sciences. A third textbook covered mid-level management of a police department. The fourth, a paperback book of fewer than one hundred pages, covered leadership styles.

"Figures," Gerald said out loud in his empty condo, "a police department like mine with poor leadership would allocate the shortest book to the topic of leadership." The remaining two books were in binder form. The first was set up as a kind of Cliffs Notes covering constitutional law: rules regarding search and seizure, suspect rights, and, just as important, exceptions to those same rights. The second binder was four inches thick and clasped within its three rings were the general orders, policies and procedures, and recent memos that had yet to be codified into the general orders for the department. *Fuck, man,* Gerald thought, *I have to cram hundreds and hundreds of pages of information and thousands of points of fact into my head in the next six weeks for a mere one hundred-question exam!* Gerald sat for several minutes staring at the mountain of information in front of him. Mentally he triaged what was most likely to be on the exam, the first step in his strategy to become a sergeant. A seventh book, the study guide, had only been cracked open by Emily.

He had been a part of hundreds of criminal investigations and been trained as an evidence technician early in his career, exposing him to many of the details the thick *Criminal Investigations* book coached. Open that book later. Gerald figured the community policing book was on the study list for political reasons, and nothing too meaty would be contained in it, and few questions from it would make the exam. Put that book last.

Gerald opened the book on leadership and read the introduction. The author had been a Marine Corps officer and decided to write his book on what makes a good leader in any field. The book revolved around the fourteen leadership traits expected of all Marines and examples of each trait in practice both in a military application and a civilian one. Gerald decided to put this book ahead of the other two. The police management book contained formulas for determining necessary personnel for a given event and monetary budget tables. *New stuff to me,* thought Gerald, *put that one next to the leadership book.* The Connecticut law enforcement handbook and the department general orders binder pretty much boiled down volumes of information into brief, practical reference paragraphs. *Those will be the first two studied, build a foundation from there.*

Gerald leaned back for a moment, allowing Emily's new cat to take the opportunity to jump on his lap. He stared at his new feline roommate, knowing he had been played by Emily when she brought it home three days earlier. "It's a rescue cat, maybe a year old," she said.

Gerald had protested, "I didn't know we wanted a cat. Besides, I'm more of a dog person."

"I'm lonely by myself on the nights you work. The cat can keep me company when you're working second and third shift. Besides, dogs are more of a commitment. Do you want me to bring something else in this house that's more of a commitment than a little cat?" she asked.

Like kids? was Gerald's immediate thought. *Hell no.* "I guess I'm a cat lover now. Cat have a name?"

"Not yet. What do you think we should call him?"

"How about 'fuckin' cat' because when it pukes in the corner, pees on the laundry, or shits on our bed, that's what we're gonna be calling it."

Emily cradled the cat like a small child and said, "How about Leonardo, Leo for short, like in law enforcement officer." She handed Gerald the cat.

He held it up, his hands under the cat's forelegs, its body hanging limp, the tip of its tail flicking back and forth. "Welcome home, Leonardo," Gerald said as he gently placed the cat on the kitchen floor. Leonardo gazed back and forth at his new roommates for a moment, then jumped onto Gerald's lap and curled up, placing his head in the open palm of Gerald's right hand. Gerald began to scratch behind Leonardo's ear.

From Leonardo's first day, Gerald started calling him

"Emily's cat" rather than "fucking cat," depriving himself of the gratification of saying "fuck," a courtesy that Emily appreciated. But right now, Emily wasn't around, and Leo kept returning to Gerald's lap looking for attention while Gerald was trying to get into a mental study mode. "Come on, you fuckin' cat, go hang out somewhere else," Gerald muttered as he stood with Leonardo in one hand. A gentle underhand toss landed Leonardo onto the carpeted living room floor. Newly distracted, he began clawing at the faded fabric of an old chair Emily had brought with her when she moved in months ago. *Not my chair,* Gerald reasoned as he sat down and popped the cap off a yellow highlighter marker. After a small exhale, he leaned over the open general orders binder and began studying.

12

Saturday
July 22
2200 hours

DONNA SAT IN THE BACK row of tables in the lineup room, which more or less resembled a classroom. She had arrived early and was waiting to see who she got as a temporary FTO. Gerald was going to be out of work today, taking a sick day at the last minute. Donna felt a little more self-conscious without Gerald as she took in the swagger and appearance of the veteran officers.

This was C squad—the evening shift of cops who started their workday at three p.m. and ended it at half-past midnight. It consisted of mostly younger officers with less than ten years on the job. There were a couple of senior guys, well into their forties or early fifties, who had over twenty years on. They generally took the nicer residential neighborhoods or desk officer assignments when possible. There was also a K9 officer, Tanner Monroe, with his German shepherd partner, Thor. Donna had heard about Tanner and Thor but had not worked with them yet due to Tanner being out for several weeks recovering from a hand injury. By three o'clock, everyone had arrived, including one old-timer, Danny Sensling, who was still tucking in his shirt and strapping on his gun belt as he sauntered into the room.

Sergeant Reilly started the lineup. "First, let's get the

district assignments done, then the lieutenant has some information to pass on."

The district assignments were almost always the same. The unwritten rule was patrol beats were assigned by seniority, with the more senior guys picking the easier beats first and the younger officers being assigned the leftover beats that were usually busier. Reilly filled out their squad sheet then turned to the lieutenant. "They're all yours, LT."

Lieutenant Cantu pulled a crumpled scrap of paper out of his shirt pocket that held his notes from the lieutenants' meeting the chief held once a week. He flattened it out and then started disseminating his notes the way he always did, by bashing the administration. "We had our lieutenants' meeting on Thursday," Cantu began, "and we started by playing BS bingo—you know, where everybody picks a favorite phrase the chief has, such as bright line, robbing Peter to pay Paul, bullet-point idea, and so on. The lieutenant who picks the phrase the chief uses the most wins the game."

Cantu continued: "Then DC Neaballa showed up ten minutes late—now, if I'd shown up ten minutes late, and being Native American and Mexican to boot, I would've been written up, but anyway DC Neaballa, who worked the street for six weeks when he first got hired and never since, starts telling us how the computers in the cruiser work fine, that it's you guys in patrol messing them up. They're also talking about putting a surveillance camera at the end of the hallway to make sure everyone is showing up and leaving when they should."

C squad was used to Cantu's ramblings and most tuned him out when he spoke. Those who did listen rarely understood what he was talking about anyway. But the mention of a surveillance camera at the end of the hallway leading to the patrol officers' locker rooms caught everyone's ear and brought a chorus of protest from the squad. Even the K9's ears perked up.

"We should be monitoring *them*, for Chrissake," came one voice from the squad.

"Who are they to see if we're coming in late or leaving early when they, and their little band of suck-ups, constantly come and go as they please?" protested another.

Cantu continued, "There will be a staff meeting in the near future where all supervisors will be invited, and you guys can put your questions in writing for the sergeants to ask at the meeting."

"These administrative assholes will analyze the handwriting on the questions and start investigating whoever wrote them," came a voice from the back of the room, drawing some laughter.

"It's true. They will," another voice agreed.

Now that the squad was partially demoralized, the lieutenant looked for a way to change the topic. He focused on Donna and said, "Donna, you've been patrolling with us for a little while now, but we don't really know you. Tell us about yourself."

"Hi, um, what do you want to know?"

"Why do you want to be a cop?" asked Sergeant Reilly.

"I want to help people."

"This isn't your oral board, and we don't believe that bullshit line anyway, so, *really,* why do you want to do this job?" asked another veteran officer.

"I thought this job would be exciting. I didn't want a nine-to-five office job, and watching CSI shows made doing police work look even more interesting."

This got some chuckles from the squad. "You're a long way from doing any CSI work," another veteran deadpanned.

"Okay, okay. Donna, have you been trained in how our K9s work?" Sergeant Reilly asked.

Donna replied, "The training sergeant gave a class with some videos during my in-house training a few weeks ago,"

"Uh-huh. Just as a refresher, Tanner, why don't you give

her a brief on what to do around the dog when we're on the street."

Before Tanner could start, Officer Cameron Canfield, known as CC to everyone, and the only African American on the squad piped up. "Tanner, your dog is racist—right now, he's giving me that look."

"He's not giving you a look," Tanner responded. "He's looking at you 'cause you're looking at him, and you always fuck with him."

"I don't fuck with him—he doesn't like me because he prejudiced."

"He's not looking at the LT, and *he's* a Hispanic."

"He doesn't like black people."

"He doesn't like people that fuck with him," Tanner said, sounding more defensive about his dog.

Tanner turned to face Donna. "The dog doesn't know race. He *does* know smells. His nose is a thousand times more sensitive than a human's, and if we're in a foot chase after a suspect, the dog is hitting off of the apocrine the suspect's body emits." Donna cocked her head slightly, and Tanner assumed she didn't understand what apocrine was. "You know, the sweat you get under your armpits like when you have to stand up in front of a crowd or in class, you get hit with a pop quiz you know you're not prepared for?" Donna nodded her head slightly. "That's emotional sweating brought on by stress, anxiety, or fear, like running from the cops. It's emitted by the apocrine glands. Its odor is distinct from sweating you get from a workout. The dog's nose is sensitive enough to pick up on that, and that's what he zeroes in on during a foot chase.

"It does help if he's familiar with you, knows your smell and your voice, so it's okay to pet him and talk to him. Just don't feed him anything. We try to keep their diet pretty strict to keep them healthy."

Donna looked at the K9 that was staring back at her,

motionless. Donna took a slow deep breath and gradually turned her eyes back to Tanner.

"If we go on a track, I usually like to have another officer with me to work the radio and give out our locations as we move so officers on the perimeter know where we're going and can adjust." He looked down admiringly at Thor and lightly scratched behind his ear. Thor ignored the attention and continued to stare at Donna.

"And whatever you do, don't ever get between me and the dog or the dog and a suspect. If you find yourself between him and a suspect, stop moving. He may stop and check you out, and he may even start to bite at you, but he'll realize pretty quick you aren't the person he wants and will start running after the suspect again."

Donna raised an eyebrow, but Tanner went on. "We've had a number of friendly biting incidents over the years, and in almost every case, the cop who was bitten messed up by getting between the handler and the dog, or they got between the suspect and the dog."

"Maybe you can use Donna as a bite dummy on a practice track later in the shift," Sergeant Reilly offered.

"Yeah, we can do that," Tanner said.

Donna wondered how she'd been volunteered, as she hadn't said a word.

"All right, Donna," Sergeant Reilly continued, "why don't you ride with Dave—we're pretty sure he's a faggot, so I'm not worried about him making a move on you."

Dave smiled and turned toward Donna, seated one row behind him, and in a voice like a drag queen said, "Hi, Donna."

"We have a motto here on C squad: There's no such thing as a stupid question. However, there are stupid people. You're going to meet a lot of stupid people out there. Be safe, and we'll see you guys at midnight," Sergeant Reilly said, ending the lineup. The squad left the room, still grousing about the idea of a surveillance camera in the hallway to monitor their comings and goings.

In the large parking lot behind the PD, Donna and Dave loaded their duty bags into their cruiser. "What stage of FTO are you in now?" asked Dave.

"I'm in third phase."

"Good, then you can drive," Dave said. "One of the most stressful things about being a patrol officer is getting a hot call and not knowing where the address is—"

"Yes, Gerald went over this with me," Donna interrupted.

Dave continued, unfazed. "Also, when you're running through backyards, pursuing someone in a foot chase, you can't check your GPS. So what you want to do is know the streets and footpaths of your beat so well that you can automatically, almost reflexively, head to a call. You know where Main and Wells is?"

"Of course, I do," replied Donna.

"Good, let's head there—you can buy me a coffee."

As Donna and Dave drove south on Main Street, a call came in about a suspicious act. The dispatcher reported a woman had observed a white male sitting next to a small playground by the Congregational church. According to the complainant, the white male, wearing a gray T-shirt and dirty jeans, was talking to different children, and maybe taking pictures with his cell phone, but didn't appear to know any of them. Dave radioed back that they were en route, as did their backup unit.

"You know where this church is, right?" Dave asked.

"By the intersection of Main Street and the Boulevard."

"Okay, good. Let's go. Code one."

Donna maneuvered the cruiser toward the intersection, which was becoming thick with traffic as rush hour started. "Just park the cruiser here on the sidewalk. I think I see him walking toward the bus stop," Dave said.

Their suspected miscreant looked left and right, then back to the ground. It looked to Donna like he was hoping to blend in with the few pedestrians in the area and not be harassed by the two cops who were now walking toward him.

Outside the bus stop enclosure, Dave and Donna caught up to their suspect. "Hey, how are you today?" Dave called out in a loud but friendly voice. Their guilty-mannered party stared at the ground and picked up his pace, anxious to put some space between him and the two cops. "Stop and talk to me, buddy. I just need to know a couple of things."

The lone white male stopped and looked at Dave. "You talking to me?"

"Yeah," Dave said, smiling.

"Well, I don't want to talk to you, and I don't have to."

Dave let out a little laugh. "Actually, yes, you do."

The suspect stood still but kept on looking to his left and right. Donna, watching the scene play out, guessed that he was looking for an avenue to escape should this encounter with law enforcement turn out not in his favor.

The smile never left Dave's face as he continued: "Word is you were talking to some of the kids by the church playground over there."

"No, I wasn't. I wasn't near there."

"Well, I observed you coming from that direction, and you fit the witness description. Why don't you tell us who you were talking to?"

"Yeah, well, who is this witness? I want to see them and tell them to their face they're full of shit."

"How about you give us your ID, for starters?"

"Fuck you."

"That's not very polite—let's see your ID."

The suspect suddenly bolted between the bumpers of two cars that were sitting in traffic. A bus in the next lane of traffic blocked his direction of travel, and in the moment he took to decide which way to run, Dave was on top of him, tackling him to the asphalt between the fenders of the vehicles. Dave started yelling, repeating, "Stop resisting—put your hands behind your back!" while at the same time landing punches to the suspect's kidneys, knocking the wind out of him.

Donna tried but couldn't get between the cars to assist

Dave. After a few long seconds, she figured out to run around the first car to get on the other side of the line of traffic. "Pin his head to the ground while I wrestle his hands behind him," Dave instructed Donna. She placed her hands on the suspect's head, which was turned sideways, and pressed down.

"You're hurting me," the suspect whined.

"Stop resisting, and you won't be hurt," Dave said loudly.

The combination of Donna's full weight on the suspect's head, along with his loss of breath, finally allowed Dave to get their man's hands behind his back and handcuffed.

"Plenty of people watching, Donna, so watch what you say and do," Dave cautioned, still grinning. "Okay, let's get him up." The officers rolled the suspect on his side and then pulled him to his feet, leading him back to the sidewalk.

Their backup officer, Danny Sensling, pulled up in his cruiser. Slowly getting out of the cruiser, he asked, "You guys all set here?"

"If you can transport him, we'll meet you at headquarters," Dave said.

"Uh, yeah, sure," Sensling replied.

Donna started to maneuver the suspect toward Sensling's cruiser when Dave called out, "Pat him down close before you put him in the cage." Donna felt slighted that Dave was telling her this, and pursed her lips, even more ticked at herself for not thinking of it first.

Donna found a wallet and cell phone on their arrestee during her pat-down, tossing them to Dave, who was a few feet away observing the process with a critical eye. As Donna double-locked the cuffs and placed their prize in the back of Sensling's cruiser, Dave fingered through the wallet, finding an identification card, giving him a name he requested dispatch to run through NCIC.

"Donald Osborne, not wanted, but he has a history of crimes against minors. Call in if you need details," came the dispatcher's voice.

"Ten-four," Dave replied. He turned on the cell phone found on Donald and navigated to the media pages. There he and Donna found multiple pictures of children at the nearby playground. Dave stepped to Sensling's cruiser and leaned in toward the back window, face to face with Donald. "This your phone?" Dave asked.

"No," Donald replied.

"Then whose is it?"

"I found it."

"When?"

"Just now."

"So you're saying this is found property, and nothing on it belongs to you?"

"That's what I'm saying."

"That's just great. Thank you, Donald. I'm sure this is all a big misunderstanding, but you're still going to jail."

"Why?"

"You ran into the travel lane of the road outside of the crosswalk and obstructed vehicular traffic. That's a class C misdemeanor, an arrestable offense that I personally witnessed. So, you have to go to jail."

Donald started yelling, "I have witnesses too. You guys beat me for no reason!"

Sensling climbed back into his cruiser, rolling up the open window so Donald's voice wouldn't attract too much attention. "We'll see you at HQ," Dave said to Sensling as he and Donna started walking back to their cruiser.

"Pop quiz: Did we have a right as police officers to stop Donald?" Dave asked Donna.

"Yes—he was in the area, he fit the description, and he was more nervous than someone should be when approached by the police."

"Good. Totality of circumstances, all that goes into the report. What will you charge him with?"

"Is there a charge for taking pictures of children?"

"Not specifically. But first, we should try to find the

witness who called it in. Even if this person doesn't want to be named in the report, I'm sure there are other details we can get from them that'll be useful. How about the cell phone—did we have a right to go into it?"

"I guess we do—I mean we did," Donna said, a bit unsure.

"Well, for a long time, it was okay. The law wasn't catching up to technology, so cops went into cell phones of arrestees and copied down incriminating information. But now we can't do that without a warrant—it's an invasion of privacy, which makes it a pain in the ass for us. So, when I asked Donald if this was his phone and he said it wasn't, that he found it, it falls under the category of found property. He has no expectation of privacy. Especially if he just found it, as he says, then there shouldn't be any of his personal info on it. So now we can go through the phone to find its proper owner, which of course will be Donald, so while conducting our duties as police officers to reunite this phone with its owner, and we come across what a reasonable person believes is evidence of a crime, then we have an obligation to determine who the criminal is and appropriately charge and arrest them," Dave said.

"Sounds good, I guess," said Donna, still not sure.

"Believe me, it's kosher. We might have to go as far as getting a warrant for his phone records, but it will be worth it. All right, let's see if we can find the witness," said Dave.

They found their witness, made their notes, and casually walked back to their cruiser. Dave said, "I probably shouldn't tell you this, but Sensling's nickname around the PD is Senseless. He's slow and barely adequate in everything he does, so just don't expect a lot out of him if he's your backup." Dave paused, then went on, "He used to be pretty good, but now he's what we call 'retired on the job.' He's just kinda worn out and tired of doing the same old thing over and over, but he has no other skills, so he keeps coming to work. Just warning ya, there will be a time, provided you pass everything and are out here on your own, that a supervisor will tell you to take over one of his cases just to get it done."

"That doesn't seem right," Donna said as she maneuvered their cruiser off the sidewalk and merged into traffic. "We all get paid the same and should be expected to do the same amount of work."

"That's the way it's supposed to work, but not how it is. The other way to look at it is we all get paid the same, whether we work hard or not. That's Sensling's attitude."

Donna pulled the cruiser up to the back door of the PD. Just as she was about to get out, Dave turned and said to her, "Don't call Sensling 'Senseless'. You haven't been around here long enough to call anyone anything but their proper name. And don't repeat what I just told you—I'm just giving you a heads-up." Donna smiled in understanding and got out.

Combining their efforts, Donna and Dave entered the phone into evidence and booked and secured Donald in his cell in less than an hour. Back in their cruiser, Dave had Donna set up at an intersection where stop sign violations were common.

"Car stops can be very boring, or very fun, or very frustrating," Dave started. "It's like a deck of cards—you never know when you're gonna pull the joker. Fifty car stops can be very routine, but one can kill you. You have no idea what's going through the mind of the operator or occupants of the vehicle until you walk up on them. One time I walked up to the operator and knocked on the window, making the hand motion to roll the window down. He looked at me, put the car in gear, and sped off, screeching his tires. Another time I stopped a woman who had a male passenger who, unbeknownst to me at the time, was a gangbanger. The gangbanger had surreptitiously opened his door and placed a loaded .38 revolver under the vehicle. My backup was sharp and noticed the gun when he got on scene. Then there are the more common occurrences like the operator arguing the ticket, threatening to call the chief, calling you an asshole. And now, with cell phones, you have to watch out that you aren't baited into saying or doing anything stupid."

"You seem more into car stops than Gerald is."

"I like to do them. Keeps me busy and makes the shift go faster. I'm lucky enough to have received extra training in performing motor vehicle interdiction stops, DUIs and such."

"What do you think about the racial profiling argument that always comes up?" Donna asked.

"Connecticut has been keeping track of motor vehicle stops for over a decade, and they haven't found a trend of racial profiling for car stops. Anecdotally, people come up with what they think is proof, but it isn't. That being said, I do know of cops who have stopped cars just because of the operator's race. It's rare, and those cops are ignorant."

Dave coached Donna on the best place to park for the crossroad they were going to monitor, where they could see the stop sign and white stop line on the pavement, but the motorists couldn't see them.

Dave continued his narrative. "No matter how often I sit here, the general motoring public will still sail through this intersection as if the stop sign isn't posted. People scream that writing traffic tickets is just a way to generate revenue for the town or police department. Some folks even think the officer writing the ticket gets a cut. None of that, of course, is even close to the truth. Any revenue generated by traffic tickets goes into the state general fund and is a drop in the bucket of the state budget. The money doesn't even come back to the PD."

Donna was anxious not to let any violators get away and kept both hands on the wheel and foot on the brake as Dave continued, "Did you know that nationally, thirty percent of all traffic fatalities are the result of speeding, and fourteen percent involve pedestrians? I don't think it's too much of a stretch to say the folks who run stop signs are probably the same ones who speed, so people who argue that we're stopping motorists for no good reason are full of it."

Donna nodded, then said, "I read a recent editorial where the writer was bashing the state police for policies regarding speeding tickets. Nowhere in the half-page article did it say anything about motorists driving too fast. It was all about supposed incentives to cops for writing traffic tickets. Seems obvious to me, if the motorists stop driving too fast and obey the traffic laws, then the cops won't have a reason to write a ticket."

"You're right. Go drive in and around L. A., California—there's a highway patrol or local cop every two miles, and everyone is doing the speed limit," Dave said. "But that way of thinking won't get you too far in this line of work. The cops get the blame when there's a fatal accident after a high-speed chase, but what's never said in the news or anywhere else is that when the police turn on the emergency lights of the cruiser, they're initiating a motor vehicle *stop*. We don't initiate the chase. The dumbass we're trying to pull over initiates the chase. The dumbass is the one who places themselves and others at risk when they drive recklessly away from the police, not the other way around. But because we, as officers, are held to a higher standard, and because the town has the deeper pockets to pay out lawsuits—which they get tired of paying—all of the liability falls on us. While we're on the topic, what's the general order regarding police pursuits?"

"I can't recite it word for word, but basically the general order asks which is greater: the risk of a pursuit or the risk of the bad guy getting away? Then there are the other conditions that come into play, like weather, time of day, speed of the pursuit, and traffic," Donna recited.

"That's pretty good. You've just reduced a fifteen-page general order down to two sentences. Let's go over some *what-ifs*. What if you get a call that a convenience store was just robbed at gunpoint and the car description matches a motor vehicle two cars in front of you? You hit the lights, and the asshole two cars up nails the gas. Pursue or not?"

"I would probably go for it."

"Good. So would I. I'll change it slightly. Same scenario, but you and the car you are pursuing are coming up to the middle school, and school just let out. Kids on the sidewalks and buses pulling out."

"I would—"

"And the cops on the scene of the robbery are calling for medical because they have the clerk on the ground suffering from a gunshot wound."

"Ummmmm . . ."

"Time's up, and *um* is not an answer. In real life, you probably won't have more than a couple of seconds to make the decision. But I'll give you some guidance. You can't undo a middle school kid being injured or killed because of the pursuit, but you can pick up the trail of the suspect at almost any time."

"So the right answer is to stop the pursuit."

"Right and hope another unit can pick it back up again in safer conditions."

"What if I were to shut down, and the bad guy still speeds through the school zone and kills a kid?"

"You'll be visiting internal affairs, and you're going to need proof that you stopped pursuing at a reasonable time. The in-car camera works for us in those cases."

Donna shook her head as she digested Dave's words. "I get it, but it doesn't seem right."

"Doesn't matter if it seems right or not. A large chunk of our society now blames the cops for suspects getting arrested, blames us when an armed suspect gets wasted by the cops, blames the cops when a fat guy high on crack and with heart problems gets Tasered and dies, you know what I mean? The fact that the fat guy snorted cocaine and busted up his house might get a sentence in the newspaper, but the

Taser use will generate three paragraphs and two follow-up articles and an op-ed railing against the cops."

Donna was nodding in agreement while staring at the intersection. She started to put the cruiser in gear after observing a compact car roll through without stopping. "Let that one go," said Dave. "Slow-rolling a stop sign isn't worth the effort to pull them over." Donna put the cruiser back in park.

Not a minute later, a minivan didn't even bother slowing down. "That's a keeper," Dave said with a smile. "Go after her. She's probably doing fifteen miles per hour through the stop sign."

Donna activated the emergency lights and pulled out behind the offending minivan, quickly catching up. Dave called in the plate number to dispatch as he and Donna continued to follow the vehicle down the street when it suddenly turned left onto a side street, then into a driveway that was barely bigger than the car. The operator, a Hispanic-looking woman of about forty-five, hurriedly exited her vehicle and started toward the front door. "Don't let her get in the house," Dave ordered. Donna was out of the cruiser quickly and managed to get up the three steps to the front door of the house at the same time as the woman, before the woman could get her keys into the lock.

"You can't keep me out of my house," the woman yelled. Donna didn't quite know what to say, but Dave was already smiling and talking.

"Lady, all we need is your driver's license, insurance card, and registration," he recited.

"*No habla ingles*," the woman replied.

"I just heard you speak English," Dave retorted. "If you don't give me your license, insurance card, and registration, I'm towing the car and arresting you."

The woman hesitated then walked back to the minivan, retrieving what Dave wanted.

"I'll write this ticket. Keep her out of the house 'til I write it up," Dave instructed Donna.

While Donna stood in front of the door, the woman got on her cell phone and started talking rapid-fire Spanish.

Dave finished writing the ticket and walked over to the woman. "Here's your ticket, ma'am. Instructions are on the back. Have a nice day." Dave then turned to Donna and said, "Let's go. We've got about two minutes before her family members show up and turn this into a circus."

As Donna k-turned the cruiser and headed back down the street, a compact vehicle with two women and several children passed. Donna watched as the car pulled up on the front lawn next to the minivan.

"There's your lesson of the day," Dave said as the women and four children exited the compact car. "Whenever someone gets on their phone, they're calling for their backup. If we were still there writing the ticket, those hens would have their phone cameras out, taking pictures and harassing the shit out of us. If we utter one wrong offhanded comment, we would be the bad guys."

"We could go back and write another ticket," Donna suggested. "At least a couple of those kids in the vehicle that just pulled up are young enough to have to be in a car seat."

"True, but fuck it. Now is not the time with them all worked up. They'll be caught another day. Pick and choose your battles."

The shift was turning out to be quiet, and Dave took the opportunity to introduce Donna to some of the denizens of his beat. "Pull in back there," Dave pointed to their left, and Donna parked their cruiser in the back lot of a three-story rooming house. "Let's take a walk and see who's around," Dave said.

The pair of cops walked up the exposed stairs to the third floor of the building. Dave took out his knife and jimmied the lock to the back door, and they entered the hallway. A faded urine odor lingered in the air as they walked to the front staircase landing. There were two residents, a man and a woman, both thin with gray hair and chin stubble. They held forty-ounce Schaeffer beers in their hands. He wore a wife-beater tank top, she had on a white T-shirt, slightly yellowed with age. The man's exposed arms showed several tattoos, all with blurred outlines and faded ink making it hard to distinguish what they were supposed to be.

"Hi guys, how's it going?" Dave said with a smile.

"Going good, officer, how are you?" Tank Top replied.

"I'm fine. Have you met Officer Harris yet?"

"No, I haven't," the man replied; the woman looked out the window and shook her head.

The male extended his hand and introduced himself. "I'm Rocky. I heard there's a new lady cop. Pleased to meet you." Donna smiled and shook his hand then glanced at the woman, expecting to repeat the greetings to her. The woman instead turned back and looked Donna square in the eye, curled her lip, shook her head, and said, "I don't like lady cops."

Rocky turned to the woman and said, "Betsy, at least you can be polite."

Betsy replied, "Fuck it. I don't want to be polite to her. I like Officer Dave. How are you, Officer Dave?"

"I'm doing quite well today, thank you, Betsy," Dave replied, then said, "any problems around here we can help you with?"

"Naw," said Rocky, "same old, same old."

"Well, we're going to continue walking around. You guys let me know if there's any trouble around here, okay?"

"We will," Rocky answered. As Donna and Dave walked down the stairs, they could hear Rocky admonishing Betsy on her manners.

They didn't find any other residents lingering around the

rooming house, so they headed back to their cruiser. "What do you think of Rocky and Betsy?" Dave asked.

"Rocky seems like he might be a character. Betsy seems like a bitch," Donna answered.

"You're right on both counts. Though I've heard Betsy is nastier to lady cops than to me or the other guys on patrol."

As Donna turned on the ignition and backed out of the lot, Dave pointed to the rooming house and said, "That place, and others like it, are the last stop people make before they start living under a bridge."

"Why do you bother going into a place like that?" Donna asked.

"Because I'm probably the only 'normal' person they encounter on a regular basis and they, in their own way, appreciate that I check on them, listen to their problems, and maybe give a little advice."

"How do you mean 'in their own way?'"

"They'll talk to me when I need information, like looking for a suspect."

Donna nodded, and Dave went on, "One of the best skills you can have in this job is to relate to everyone regardless of their social status. Don't come off as high and mighty during casual conversations with citizens. And in case you haven't figured it out yet, the clean-cut middle-class folks aren't rubbing elbows with too many criminals. The Rockys and Betsys of the town are. Oftentimes, they're the ones who know what's going on in the dark corners of my beat."

Dave smiled and said, "Don't you find it ironic that they knew about you, the new lady cop, but you didn't know anything about them?"

Donna said, "I have noticed that everyone will look at a cruiser going down the street. They've probably seen me driving with Gerald."

"That's my point. They have eyes and ears. They just need someone to talk to and ask the right questions once in a while. In this beat, that someone is me."

The radio calls were slow for the shift, and Dave spent most of their time going from one coffee shop and rooming house to another chatting up the inhabitants of his beat, many of whom represented a section of the population most people would go out of their way to avoid. Dave had an easy manner about him that elicited warm greetings in each encounter. Donna made a mental note to try to emulate Dave. Be a friend to those who are down and out or a little bit weird. Maybe make up for that lost chance years ago in high school.

———————————

At 2332 hours, they were about to head in to headquarters and unload their cruiser when they heard Tanner's voice over the radio. "Unit Thirty-Two, I've got an Acura occupied four times with a misuse plate. Prospect Street heading toward the Boulevard. Just lit them up, and they're not stopping."

"Ten-four. Any units nearby?" the dispatcher replied.

"Unit Twenty-One, we're coming up behind them," Dave said into their cruiser mic, then turned to Donna. "Hit it. They should be right around the next curve. I'll work the lights, siren, and radio. You just keep Tanner in sight."

Donna hit the gas as the blue and red emergency lights from the cruiser reflected off street signs and buildings. Tanner's cruiser was now only a hundred feet in front of them, also with its emergency lights on. Donna could also hear Tanner's siren wailing.

"They're not stopping and are increasing their speed . . . west on Prospect." Tanner coolly stated.

"Unit Twenty-One, we'll call direction and travel . . . we're behind Thirty-Two—stay with him, Thirty-Two," Dave stated into his radio. Donna kept her cruiser about three car lengths behind Tanner, alternately mashing the gas pedal and brake as the three vehicles sped at full throttle on short straight sections of roads, then braked heavily at the corners. Dave had activated their siren. The engine screamed on each acceleration and was beginning to emanate a burnt oil smell. The tires squealed, and the old cruiser fishtailed badly on one corner, but Donna recovered. So far, Sergeant Reilly had remained silent; the chase could continue.

The Acura didn't head onto the highway the way most fleeing suspect vehicles did, but instead headed into the Meadows, an area of warehouses and small businesses where the streets were formed into neatly squared blocks and only two roads led in or out.

"This is about as good as it's going to get for a car chase," Dave said. "It's late, there are no pedestrians or vehicles around, and our backup units will cover the two roads leading out of here. In other words, this chase will end down here. These assholes have nowhere to go."

Donna stayed close to Tanner's cruiser, her eyes focused, her hands and feet reacting to every weave and dip the car in front of her made. The Acura darted left, suddenly jumping the curb and sped across a small lawn, crashing through a short metal gate, and heading up a dirt road leading to the top of the river dike. The dike was a thirty-foot-high man-made structure bordered on one side by a swamp and the other by the Meadows business district. A steep slope led down both sides. Tanner followed, kicking up a dust cloud as his tires spun on the loose dirt. Donna jumped the curb and kept up with Tanner, his emergency lights now fuzzy red and blue flashes in the dust cloud. Dave called in the action over the radio. All three vehicles bounced and shuddered on the dirt road.

"Get ready for a foot chase," came someone's voice over the radio. As if on cue the Acura turned right, sliding down the slope of the dike, dust and dirt kicking up from under it as all four wheels braked hard; the driver had lost control and couldn't avoid crashing with a metallic *bang* into a large metal dumpster located behind a warehouse. Within the dust cloud, four doors of the wrecked Acura flew open, and four shadows fled in different directions. Streetlights and security lights on building rooftops, along with cruiser headlights and flashing emergency lights, destroyed everyone's night vision, making the running shadows almost invisible and obstacles impossible to see.

Tanner ground his cruiser to a halt on top of the dike. Donna jammed on her brakes as hard as she could as her cruiser skidded at an angle to a stop inches from Tanner's rear bumper. Donna almost forgot to put the cruiser in "park" as she flung open her door and ran behind Dave, who had begun to run down the dike. Tanner had let Thor loose and was a half step ahead of Dave, commanding, "GET HIM!" repeatedly to his K9 partner. The German shepherd instantly zeroed in on the closest fleeing dark silhouette, now the dog's prey, closing in as the suspect sprinted into the darkness behind a neighboring warehouse. Just as Thor's target was going to make the corner of the building, the dog lunged and locked his jaws onto the right calf of the runner. The K9 and his prey tumbled to the ground. Thor never broke his crushing bite even as he was being kicked in the head by his captured criminal. Canine instincts took over the dog as it violently shook his head and body back and forth, ripping the muscle tissue his teeth were buried in. The downed felon's senses were being overloaded. Loud voices and lights filled his ears and eyes. Pain had not set in yet. The weight of the beast clutching his leg kept him from standing. He was living the nightmare of wanting to run, but his right leg wouldn't move. Desperately kicking and crawling, the felon wanted to escape. He gave one more desperate effort to free himself before his nose exploded in pain and blood.

"Don't kick the dog, motherfucker," Dave shouted as he swung his metal flashlight into the shadow's nose with a flick of his forearm.

"Break! Break!" Tanner yelled, commanding Thor to let loose his bite.

"We got this one," Dave said to Tanner. "Go sniff out the others."

Tanner put Thor on a leash and was heading back to the Acura to let Thor sniff out the scents of the other three suspects. Donna and Dave cuffed their suspect and frisked him before pulling him to his feet. "My leg hurts!" cried the suspect. "I can't walk."

"Just walk with us to the curb in front of this building, then you can sit," Dave ordered.

"Your police dog didn't have to bite me!"

"You didn't have to run. You could've stayed in the car. While we're on that topic, why did you guys drive away from us?"

"I don't know—I wasn't driving. My leg really fucking hurts. Is my nose bleeding?"

"I'm sure it does, and yes, you have a bloody nose. Sit here." Dave took a good look at their suspect now that they were under a streetlight, *a high school kid, for sure.* Dave had the teenager sit down on the curb on the edge of a small parking lot, took out his notepad and pen and asked, "What's your name and date of birth?" The teenager gave him the information as he began rocking back and forth in pain.

Over their portable radios, Donna and Dave heard Tanner and his K9 track for one of the other suspects. "K9 is pulling hard . . . heading east along the bottom of the dike through the brush." Tanner and Thor became one, the K9 and handler physically and metaphorically tied together by the leather lead, each interpreting the other's moves, unconsciously reacting to the other's rate of respiration, body language, pitch of voice or growl. Thor wanted the animalist thrill of taking down prey with a bite. Tanner wanted the thrill of capturing a thief on the run.

Tanner jogged, managed Thor's leash, talked on the radio, and got smacked in the face by unseen branches all at the same time in the dark. Between heaving breaths,

Tanner said, "I observed two suspects run this way, east, when they crashed." Upon hearing this, two officers shifted their perimeter several buildings to the east, paralleling and ahead of Tanner's track.

An abrupt movement was felt more than it was seen or heard.

"Police. Don't move!" Tanner commanded the dark figure hiding between a stack of wood pallets and the cinderblock wall of a warehouse. "Come toward me with your hands out in front." Thor was pulling on his lead, barking ferociously. Tanner commanded the K9: "Dooown!" The dog lay down on his stomach. The figure tentatively stepped toward Tanner and Thor, who was still barking intensely, his sprays of dog spittle reflecting in Tanner's flashlight beam. "Lay down on your belly, hands out to the sides," Tanner further commanded the suspect, who slowly complied.

The two officers who had been paralleling and ahead of Tanner suddenly appeared out of the dark, stumbling through thick brush. "There's got to be another one nearby," Tanner said.

"Where's your friend?" one of the officers asked the figure on the ground as he leaned down to place the kid in handcuffs.

"I don't know. Why you chasing me?" was the reply.

"Because we like chasing dumb motherfuckers, and you're about as stupid as they come," the officer replied as he cinched up the cuffs.

"There's still two more," Tanner repeated. "I want to get all four of them."

"Here's the third one," the second officer said. "Come on out of there, asshole. You decide to run, the dog will bite you." Tanner looked to his left to see the uniformed officer standing on top of a five-gallon bucket, holding his flashlight so the beam pointed down into a dumpster just a few feet away. The suspect inside the dumpster climbed out, keeping his hands where the cops could see them.

Sergeant Reilly had arrived where the Acura had crashed and was coordinating the scene, which was fluid with one suspect still on the run. "Widen the perimeter," he said automatically, but he knew in his mind the perimeter was breaking down. With only eight units—meaning eight police bodies—half were already tied up frisking and babysitting the three already captured. Knowing Tanner lived for a good K9 track and wouldn't give up without capturing all four suspects, Reilly added, "and someone run with the K9 while they continue their track."

Tanner had brought Thor back to the Acura one more time for a fresh scent and was now heading off to the west at a jog behind the leashed K9. A second patrol officer jogged with him.

Reilly looked at the Acura and then at Sensling, who stood nearby serving no purpose. "Danny, let's you and I toss the Acura. See what we can find."

The Acura had been driven hard, the engine had stalled, but the ignition warning was still ringing its annoying bing-bong noise as Reilly and Sensling began their task. The interior was still neat, save for the deployed airbags, which made the brown paper lunch bag sticking out from under the back of the driver's seat that much more noticeable. Reilly reached for the bag and looked inside, observing a black semiautomatic handgun. "Forty to Unit Thirty-Two," Reilly said into his radio, "be advised we found a semiautomatic handgun in the Acura."

Tanner's backup responded for him. "Roger. We're continuing to track west and south, up toward the car dealership."

Without saying so out loud, Reilly had just let everyone know the *plus one* rule was in effect. The plus one rule simply meant there was always one more weapon than what had been found. Cops had been killed believing that, upon finding one weapon at a scene, they'd found the *only* weapon, realizing too late they'd relaxed too early when a second unsecured weapon was used against them. Tanner and his backup now considered the suspect they were tracking as armed until they proved otherwise.

Three blocks away, Tanner followed his K9 partner, who was still pulling hard but now doubling back and forth along the edge of a tall cyclone fence topped with razor wire. "The breeze is starting to mess up the scent. That's why we're going in a circle," Tanner lamented to his backup. "Let's double back and try one more time." Tanner and Thor gave it another try, but the wind had picked up, and one of their squadmates had driven the block a couple of times, further disturbing the air and any scents for Thor's sensitive nose.

Suspect number four got away. At least for now.

Their tracking responsibilities complete, Tanner secured Thor in the rear of his cruiser and carefully backed down the dirt road from the top of the dike, making a mental note of the damage done to the gate at the beginning of the access road. Driving the two blocks back to the scene of the crash, he began to go through his mental checklist of what needed to be done: Have the Acura towed and contents inventoried, run the Vehicle Identification Number and try to locate the owners, fill out a use-of-force form, fill out a K9 bite form, drive to the emergency room and photograph the injury to the suspect Thor had bitten, interview and try to get statements from each of the three suspects, secure the gun found in the Acura and run the serial number, write a request for the gun to be checked for prints by evidentiary, book three prisoners, and, finally, write the arrest report before the suspects went before a judge at ten in the morning.

Sergeant Reilly walked up to Tanner. "It's the end of the shift, so everyone will take on a responsibility to help you with this case. Your main work will be the report and use-of-force documentation. What tipped you off to these assholes, anyway?"

"Towns around here have been getting hit with a lot of stolen Acuras. Assholes steal the Acuras and take the engine out, then put them in their Hondas and race them. There's a whole underground racing circuit doing this. I saw the Acura, ran the plate—it came back stolen, and off we went."

"Nice work. By the way, the gun was found under the driver's seat, but easily accessible to all four occupants. I'll note that in my portion of the report, but it's safe to charge all of them with the possession of a firearm charge. Maybe one of them will rat out another, and we can get them to work off each other."

"I'll try to sit with each of them and see what I can get."

Donna and Dave followed the flatbed tow truck hauling the Acura to the police department impound lot, where they carried out their assignment of inventorying the contents of the vehicle. "This is easy work," said Dave as he noted items located in the glove box, "we get a little overtime and also save Tanner about a half-hour so he can concentrate on more important parts of the case." Turning to Donna, who knelt outside the driver's door peering under the seat with her flashlight, he asked, "Was that your first car chase?"

"Yup."

"What did you think of it?"

"It was fun, exciting—kinda couldn't believe it was happening at first."

"You did good. First rule is don't get in an accident and wreck your own cruiser. Maintain control. You did that. Do you remember the radio traffic during the chase?"

"Some of it. I knew you were working the radio, so I didn't really listen as close."

"It comes with experience, but you need to drive fast but safely, listen and talk on the radio, and think tactically. You did good by stopping on top of the dike and letting the suspects drive down the slope on their own. We would've definitely fucked up our cruiser, and probably been injured if we'd followed. Any questions on the apprehension of the first suspect—the one bit by the K9?" Dave was fishing to see if Donna felt comfortable with the flashlight smack he'd landed on the suspect's face. It was rare, but some new recruits had a more liberal view of how suspects should be treated and had made complaints up the chain of command.

"He made his choices. He can take his lumps," said Donna with a shrug.

"My thoughts exactly. A suspect punching or kicking a police dog warrants a return punch and or kick. And don't for a second think that those four shitheads didn't want to see us get into an accident and injured. They were hoping for just that. Imagine the street cred they would get if one of us was killed chasing them? Make no doubt in your mind, we're considered the enemy in every criminal's mind, large and small. They're out to hurt you."

Dave continued, "Reminds me of a state trooper I met in a training class years ago. He told a story over lunch where he was new and riding with an experienced trooper, and they got into a chase, much like we did tonight. Only in the trooper's case, it was just the two of them in one cruiser with no other backups. It was a long, dangerous chase, and the suspect finally crashes, bad. The experienced trooper gets out of his cruiser and walks up to the suspect driver, who's pinned in the wreck and pretty fucked up, leans down into the guys face, and says, 'Fuck you, you piece of shit. You wanted me dead back there, but I'm not, and I'm going to wait a few minutes to call for an ambulance just so you can think about that.'" Dave was still smiling as he summarized, "That's a little extreme, but it's personal between us and the bad guys. These guys wanted to see us hurt tonight."

Donna said a soft "uh-huh" as she shuffled through some paperwork from the center console, and Dave wasn't sure if he sounded too much like a thug. He continued. "A dog bite and a little beatdown, I mean, shit, that kid we caught

128

never said, 'Don't hurt me,' or 'I give up,' or 'Please stop.' The only thing that stopped him was overwhelming physical force and pain. If it wasn't for the dog and a little kiss to his nose, he'd still be running and stealing cars tomorrow. They challenged us to a fight and lost. Remember, there's no second place in a street fight."

Donna remained quiet as she peered with her flashlight under the seats and into the various compartments of the Acura, reconciling in her mind that Dave, the same guy who befriends the downtrodden and weird, can, when necessary, become momentarily violent toward another person, switching moments later to become casually calm and accommodating.

"I get it," Donna said. "Remember, I'm being trained by Gerald, who doesn't appear too slow to reach out and touch someone."

Dave said, "Yeah, he's old school."

13

Monday
July 24
1000 hours

IN-SERVICE TRAINING IS A PAIN in the ass for each and every officer, who is mandated by the state to undergo forty hours each year. Sergeant Mitch Reilly was in no hurry to attend the latest class, which fell under the umbrella of diversity training. With over twenty-four-and-a-half years on the job, he was counting the hours until retirement. Over two decades ago, his wife quit working after their first child was born. A second child and a single paycheck directed Reilly's career path—make sergeant and grab all the overtime he possibly could. Working the extra hours each week, usually the midnight patrol shift, didn't bother him. He believed his obligation to his marriage was to provide, and his wife's was to nurture. Faded Sarah Palin bumper stickers decorated Reilly's equally faded Chevy truck. There had been some lean times, but it worked for his family. Now that his kids were out of the house, Reilly and his wife felt less tied down and began exploring the option to move out of Connecticut, with its three hundred and fifty taxes and fees weighing down its citizens, to a saner, cheaper, and more conservative state. Maybe one of the Carolinas. If he was lucky, they would move before the new proposed highway tolls got enacted.

Loath to attend the class, a makeup day no less because he had missed his scheduled training, Mitch had procrastinated. Now, late to the classroom, he had to sit in the front row as the dayshift platoon and a couple of midnight guys, here on their regularly scheduled training day, had filled in most of the seats from the back of the room forward in typical cop fashion.

Mitch looked around, observing a thin, thirty-something light-skinned black female with a red-tipped white cane wedged between her thigh and the arm of her chair, sitting at the front of the classroom. Next to her was a college-age woman with a book bag and a large stack of pamphlets. *A blind instructor*, Mitch thought, *no PowerPoint presentation today.* The young woman, the instructor's assistant, was a pretty redhead but seemed to dress and act in a mannish style. If her goal was to diminish any first-impression charm, she succeeded. *Dressing like a man doesn't make you one,* Mitch thought.

The assistant whispered in the instructor's ear. The class was about to start. "Hello everyone, I'm Professor Claudia Densmore. I teach at Mountain State College in Vermont, where I have been instructing classes on diversity and community relations for ten years. This is my assistant, Rosemary, who is interning for me."

Claudia continued, "We're here today to talk about diversity and how police respond to cultures that are different than the ones they grew up in, and how your values may not match up with those of whom you serve. Does anyone here think those differences make it harder to relate to the citizens of your community?"

The question was met with dead silence. Mitch, whose seat was in the first row on the end, leaned back, turning his head to survey the room behind him.

An outsider might expect the students of this class to be slightly uncomfortable with a blind/minority instructor, or to have some sympathy to go along with the topic of discussion. An outsider would have been very wrong. This dayshift patrol squad was made up of a mix of senior officers, most of whom had more than twelve years on the job. Several had twice that. Many of the twenty officers in this room had been rotated through the detective bureau, juvenile crimes, SWAT, narcotics, internal affairs, and administrative jobs. They had been around to see this town go from a blue-collar, predominately Caucasian working town to a mix of every race. This wasn't Sergeant Mitch Reilly's assigned squad. But he knew most of the officers well, and they knew him. A couple of the old-timers in the last row looked toward Mitch. They knew what was coming from their Sarah-Palin-loving conservative sergeant who was now looking at Professor Claudia with his head slightly cocked and the skin under his bad comb-over turning red.

The professor tried again: "I grew up the daughter of two schoolteachers, so education was a big part of my family. It helps to understand the world around you."

A voice from the middle of the room responded. "So what you're saying is if you're uneducated, you can't relate to or understand the world you live in? And because you're in front of a room full of cops, my guess is you're saying we're uneducated, and for that reason, we don't relate well to our community?"

"Your police department is one of ten in the state that has a high ranking of motor vehicle stops in which minorities are pulled over a disproportionate amount of times compared to how many minorities live in this town," the professor responded coolly. "Perhaps understanding why this happens . . . if this practice is unfair, that demographic will begin to feel as if they are being oppressed."

"Oppressed! *Oppressed*," Officer Steve Kleinfelter exclaimed. "I'm Jewish, lady. Don't for a second sit there and use that word and expect some sympathy because we're pulling over and writing tickets to more than our fair share of minorities. You want to talk about oppressed: the Jews have been oppressed for two thousand years. Five hundred years ago, Jews were walled off and guarded in a section of Venice they called a ghetto. That word has stuck ever since."

The professor's expression didn't change, and Steve continued. "A refugee boat full of Jews from Germany was turned away from the United States in the late thirties and sent back to Germany. You do know what happened *there*, don't you? Are we crying about that? Demonstrating in the streets? No." Steve looked around his fellow officers with a wry smile on his face. "This lady thinks she knows what oppressed means."

"Maybe I used the wrong word, but you should understand where someone without your upbringing is coming from," the professor said.

The scalp under Mitch's bad comb-over had gone from light red to full-on crimson, a sign to all who knew him that he was about to come uncorked. He said, "I don't know what to say, lady. Stealing is stealing. Assault is assault. Rape is rape. And sex with a young girl or boy is wrong in any culture or context. We don't need to know about a person's fucked-up reason for committing the crime. We try to prevent the crimes from happening and pick up the pieces when they do. All we need to know is what degree of charges to bring against the assholes we arrest. It sounds like what *you* want us to do is turn the other way when we see abnormal and illegal behavior and pretend it's normal."

Claudia appeared unruffled. "What about car stops and the stop and frisk that some of your officers do? How many of those are based on a person's color or the neighborhood they're in? Many blacks and Hispanics feel they are targeted as soon as they walk out the door. Many towns and cities have the same problem with small minorities being targeted for confrontations with the police."

"You have it wrong, lady." Mitch was letting loose, jabbing his index finger into the table in front of him with each fact he spat out. "We don't target minorities—they target themselves. Our country had one hundred thousand black-on-black murders in the last fifteen years. And as far as we cops are concerned, we're six times more likely to be killed by someone black than the reverse. And just so it's clear, lady, we don't make up the description of a suspect. The victim does, and since more victims are describing black or Hispanic perpetrators, it's only natural that we interact more with citizens of those races."

"You tell 'em, Sarge!"

"If we did things your way, by having our street stops reflect our town's demographics, half of our street stops would be women because they represent half the town. That wouldn't be doing an awful lot to prevent or solve crimes, now, would it?"

"Many minorities feel they're treated like a suspect just because of their race. 'Driving while black' is the common complaint," said Claudia.

Another voice came from the back of the room. "I challenge you to figure out the race and gender of the operator of any vehicle while driving behind it. Sun glare on the windows makes it nearly impossible to see through them, and besides, most vehicles now have tints on the rear window and back doors. The fact is, professor, most of the time, we don't know who's in a vehicle until we walk up to the car door."

"But your town has an increase of minority car stops at night, and one study showed police would observe the race of a person operating a vehicle by using your headlights from a cross street and then pull them over."

Mitch jumped in again, "That study sounds like anti-cop bullshit, professor. We set up in areas where there's more criminal activity. For example, more drug dealing occurs in poorer neighborhoods with a higher concentration of minorities. Drugs get to these neighborhoods by motor vehicles operated by minorities. So please, tell me, who are we going to stop?"

Claudia answered, "What if a white person is driving into this same neighborhood?"

"Well, that's a slam dunk, lady! That's a customer looking to score some drugs. Of course, he gets stopped!"

Rosemary jumped into the conversation eager to vindicate and protect her professor, "So, you *do* stop people based solely on their color!"

"No, honey. That's not how it works," Mitch said, knowing by calling a man-dressing leftist woman 'honey' would piss her off. Mitch slowed the cadence of his speech as if he was talking down to a five-year-old child. All the officers in the room were enjoying the derisive tone of his mini-lecture. "The police can use a motor vehicle violation as a pretext to stop a car and interview the operator. To dumb this down for you, let's say our white male driver is in a drug-dealing neighborhood at an odd hour. He rolls through a stop sign, or forgets to use his turn signal, or he's weaving, or on his phone. All are legitimate reasons to pull him over. From there, the officer can write him a ticket or written warning for the violation, and also ask some questions, like who he's looking for or why he is there, and then observe the guy's body language. How nervous is he, is he sweating, is his voice shaky, et cetera. The officer might get nothing more, but he also might get permission to search the vehicle or the driver's pockets. These very same tools have netted us countless drugs and guns. One time we even caught two mules driving from New Mexico with eight pounds of weed in the trunk."

Mitch leaned forward his chair. "I would think, since you're from a college in Vermont, a state where opioid use is rampant, you would want the police to be interdicting the illegal drug trade. Yes?" Mitch asked.

"Opioid addiction is an illness," Claudia responded.

"Yes, it is," Mitch countered, "but are you going to tell me that every addict in Vermont started out with a prescription from a doctor for pain?"

"Well—" Rosemary began.

Mitch held up his hand, palm to Rosemary, whose

mouth was open and ready to spill out counterpoints. Mitch continued, "I doubt it because most of the addicts were young and healthy before they started abusing drugs. But prescription drugs are legal, accepted—and they are abused. Kids with ADHD sell their Adderall and Ritalin to their classmates and college kids buy the same drugs to help them focus and retain the information they learn in class because that's what Adderall and Ritalin do."

"But—"

"Drug use is accepted in this country when the drugs come from a doctor, which makes sense, but drug abuse is becoming accepted because we now label it an illness, and if it's an illness, then the drug abuse is not the fault or responsibility of the abuser. Right?"

"That's not—"

Mitch cut off Rosemary again. "For example, decriminalizing marijuana further moves the line of acceptance closer to more people, who would not otherwise use weed, and they start using—thereby increasing the number of people using drugs. Is that what you ladies want?"

Claudia recited her well-worn line, "Decriminalizing marijuana means fewer minorities getting locked up by the police."

"Another line of bullshit. Now try to keep up with me as I explain how things really work. Decriminalizing weed actually helps the illegal drug dealers. They sell their weed for less than the legitimate marijuana stores do and occasionally sprinkle it with ketamine. So all of your new users now go to the illegal dealers to buy cheaper and more powerful weed. This means the criminal gangs—the ones making money off prostitution and sex trafficking of minors and illegal aliens and dealing hardcore drugs and cheap marijuana—are profiting off of your stupid liberal arts ideals—and those are the ones we put in jail."

"But that's not—"

"No buts about it. I'll put it so you ladies can understand

it—the Dutch legalized marijuana in 1976. Twenty years later, there was a three hundred percent increase in use by teenagers. Guess who deals with the result of your fucked-up policies? We do. The police."

Kleinfelter chimed in, "The Sarge listens to every conservative radio and TV talk show there is, lady, so he's gonna spit out every fact he knows and bury you under them. I think what the Sarge is saying is that it's accepted by our society for a person to decide to try an illicit drug." There were grunts of agreement in the classroom. Kleinfelter added, "A drug that is illicit because our fellow citizens have deemed it dangerous to ingest. A drug that anyone with intelligence knows can harm them and maybe kill them but at the very least make them a burden to their fellow citizens." He paused, leaned forward in his chair, and asked, "Please tell me, why do people take such a stupid first step?"

Before Claudia or Rosemary could respond, other members of the platoon started giving their own answers:

"Because they're losers!"

"Because they're fucked up!"

"Because they live in Vermont!"

"Because they go to your college!"

"Because they take your class!" The platoon was laughing now and on a roll.

Claudia sat impassively, Rosemary was red-faced, and her hands were starting to shake. *The conversation had gone from a debate to personal*, Mitch thought. *Claudia's whole goal here was to paint the cops as the bad guys, and she had her ass handed to her. She really shouldn't have fucked with a platoon of cops who, by the very nature of their job, didn't back down from confrontation. And she shouldn't have fucked with me!*

The training sergeant, whose office was just off the classroom, stuck his head in to ask what the commotion was about. A voice from the back of the room called out, "Hey Sarge, do we have to listen to any more of this shit?"

Mitch made eye contact with the training sergeant, Paul Walsh, shook his head and made a cutting motion across his neck, mouthing, *take a break.*

"Be back by 1300," Paul said loudly. The room was empty in thirty seconds.

Mitch walked into Paul's office, sat down in a rolling chair that didn't roll, its wheels having flat spots, and put his feet up on the desk. Mitch and Paul had become trusted friends years earlier when Mitch was Paul's FTO. Since that time, Paul had used Mitch, who was five years further along in his career, as a sounding board on how to navigate the obstacles in a law enforcement career. Now with nearly eighteen years on the job himself, Paul sometimes found himself advising Mitch.

Paul said, "I could hear the commotion and some of the comments before I stuck my head in. . . . That was a pretty fucked-up class."

"Sure was," Mitch said.

Paul said, "The administration here or, for that matter, everywhere in this country, is under pressure to prove that the police aren't cowboys. This was our admin's way of trying to show the politicians and critics we're progressive. It'll be on our records that everyone attended the class and are therefore properly trained, even though we didn't learn anything new about diversity. On the flip side of the coin, I think we broadened Professor Claudia and Intern Rosemary's view of the world."

"Yeah, now they hate cops even more," replied Mitch.

"I think I get where the professor was trying to go, though. If I ask you where your family's from, what your heritage and traditions are, what would you say?"

"I'm fourth-generation Irish. Both sides of my family came from County Cork during one of the potato famines.

We drink, we fight, and all the girls take Irish step classes," said Mitch.

"See, *you* know that, but an African American doesn't. Their country of origin, their heritage, isn't there. It makes a difference."

"So African Americans are supposed to get a pass on committing crimes?

"No, of course, I'm not saying that. Just trying to show a different point of view. Maybe they, the African Americans, are saying 'you caused this.'"

"Caused what?"

"The environment they're in."

"Me and my family didn't cause anything."

"Again, not saying that. But we, as police officers, represent the government and all of its policies, past and present."

"Not sure I buy that, but whatever."

After a moment, Mitch came back to the lecture. "You do know the professor was all but saying we're racist, and she tried to prove that by bringing up the motor vehicle stop statistics."

"I know," Paul said. "I also know of an officer—since retired—who would pull over vehicles just based on the driver's race. Many years ago, not long after I completed FTO, I doubled up with him, and he pulled over a car with two Hispanics in it. They hadn't committed any violations, but this cop actually said to me that they were Spanish, and in our town, so they must've been up to no good. As he's getting out of the cruiser to approach them, he turned to me and said, 'I'll tell them they have a broken taillight.' I'm thinking to myself, *What is this, Mississippi in the sixties*? He talked to the operator, didn't write a ticket, and we cleared the stop with a verbal warning. That was the last time I ever rode with him. And you know CC on evening shift? He gets pulled over in the town he lives in a couple of times a month. And it's always by the same cop. You can't help but think if CC were white, would he be getting pulled over at all?"

"So, of all the cops you know and worked with over the years, those are the only two instances of race-based citizen contact?" Mitch asked.

"Yup. I suppose if you were going to put a number on it, it would be something like less than one percent. But it's those small number of cops that are fucking it up for the rest of us."

Paul's phone rang, and he answered it. Mitch sat in silence, ignoring the phone conversation Paul was having and stared at a poster on the wall that said, "Put a poorly trained officer on the street, and something will happen. Probably something bad."

Paul hung up the phone and said, "I'm gonna help the blind professor pack up and send her on her way, which means you get a couple of hours to kill before the next class."

"Sounds good," Mitch responded. "What's the topic of the next class going to be?"

"The Ferguson Effect."

"Are the instructors for or against cops?"

"One is retired FBI, and the other is a retired chief from somewhere in the Midwest."

"A fed and a chief. That could go either way."

"Be in the classroom by one o'clock and find out."

"I'll be there. By the way, what happened to the wheels of this chair?"

Paul smiled and said, "Well, you know how we have some rather heavy people in dispatch?"

"Yeah."

"That chair came from there. I found it in the hall outside the dispatch room with the words 'I can't take it anymore' on a piece of paper taped to it. Apparently, someone's fat ass is so heavy their weight prevented the wheels from turning, so they got ground down dragging against the floor."

Mitch was going to make a comment, but instead just smiled and left the room.

14

Monday
July 24
1244 hours

MITCH ARRIVED AT THE CLASSROOM fifteen minutes early this time so he could secure a seat in the back row. Two men in suits were at the front of the classroom, setting up for a PowerPoint presentation. Mitch was skeptical of the instructors. Any federal law enforcement officer he had worked with always believed in sharing information—meaning the local cops should share it with the feds, who wouldn't reciprocate the favor. It had gotten better after 9/11, but it still wasn't a two-way street. And chiefs, well, Mitch had to respect their rank, but it was hard to respect too many of them.

The classroom filled up, and the first instructor started with his introduction. "Good afternoon everyone, I'm retired Special Agent Victor Allen. I served in the FBI for twenty-five years and am currently an adjunct instructor at the FBI Academy. My experience was in white-collar crime and some RICO cases, until 9/11, when I was moved over to intelligence, focusing on domestic terrorism. Since I retired two years ago, I've been focusing on domestic policing policies, teaching several classes to local law enforcement officers who are selected to attend Quantico. My fellow instructor today is Chief Don Davies from Hillsdale, Illinois."

Chief Davies stepped forward. "Hello, everyone. Just a

brief introduction—I've been in law enforcement thirty years, chief the past four. I understand this morning's class was short and maybe a little contentious?"

"You could say that," came a voice from Mitch's left, followed by another closer to the front. "It sucked."

Davies continued. "Well, I hope this class won't suck. Victor and I are here to talk about what's happening in our country today. How the police are viewed. The role of the media. We want you to be honest with yourselves about how you go about doing your job. You don't have to say anything out loud, but we do want you to think.

"First thought topic," Davies said. "How do you view yourselves as police officers? Past classes have said protectors of the community, crime solvers, social workers . . . Anybody have their own view?"

"Social workers with a gun . . . that we sometimes have to use," came a reply.

"I like that," Davies continued, "because we all know most of the work we do *is* social work. Mediating neighbor disputes and keeping the peace. Checking on suspicious acts that are figments of the complainants' imaginations. Writing traffic and parking tickets. Directing traffic. Writing arrest warrants for bad checks. Filling out accident reports, which are really forms for the state and insurance companies to gather statistics from. Finding lost children or senior citizens. Investigating computer crimes. None of these activities requires a gun. A majority of police officers will never fire their gun at a person in their entire career.

"Now, how do you think the public views the police?" Davies asked.

"That depends," came an answer from the middle of the classroom. "Some like us, some hate us. I guess you could say we are a necessary nuisance."

Another voice said, "I'm sure there are some there who are happy when a cop goes down. Or are at least ambivalent about it, figuring we signed up for a dangerous job and line-of-duty deaths are a part of it."

Mitch didn't feel it, but his heart rate and blood pressure ticked up as he listened to the conversation.

Davies nodded. "Yes, they like us when we catch the bad guy, but they hate us when we pull them over for speeding or running a stop sign, often asking, 'Why aren't we out catching real criminals?' And I'm sure most of you are aware of some citizens going on social media to gloat about their despicable actions against the police."

Davies pulled out a notecard and read from it. "Here's one such Twitter post. 'Pistol whipped his ass to sleep.' That one, from Alabama, came from a suspect who had beaten a cop unconscious with the officer's own gun during a car stop. The officer later said he had refrained from using force to defend himself for fear of media backlash. Here's another: Protesters in St. Paul chanting, 'Pigs in a blanket, fry 'em like bacon.' That came a day after Houston Sherriff's Deputy Darren Goforth was assassinated while filling up his cruiser's gas tank."

Davies continued the grim count. "Going back to June 2014, two white supremacists, a male and female, shot and killed two officers who were seated in a restaurant in Las Vegas. The suspects reportedly yelled, 'This is a revolution.' They killed themselves in a Walmart a short distance away when responding officers arrived.

"September 2014: Two Pennsylvania state troopers were shot at night in the barracks parking lot. One was wounded and survived; one died. The assailant was a white male, a self-styled survivalist. He was caught forty-eight days later.

"December 2014: Two NYPD detectives were shot and killed while sitting in their patrol car. Before the murders, the killer posted anti-police threats on Instagram: 'I'm putting wings on pigs today, they take one of ours, let's take two of theirs,' an apparent reference to the police-involved deaths of Eric Garner and Michael Brown. He used the hashtag *shootthepolice*. Obviously, there are more," Davies said, "but I don't need to continue to make the point."

There was quiet in the room. The veteran officers, the ones who had been on the job over fifteen years, knew the acute pain of a fallen brother. Each mention of an officer killed in the line of duty picked at an old wound that had mostly healed over but still left a scar. For one or two of the veterans, including Mitch, that scar was still sore to the touch.

Allen picked up on the lecture. "According to Community Oriented Policing Services—part of the Department of Justice—ambush suspects were disproportionally non-white, from a lower socioeconomic status and unemployed. It seems obvious the same suspects were from a lower-income neighborhood."

Allen brought up the first PowerPoint slide. "A review of sixty-six police killers in 2013 and 2014 noted that while a majority of assailants had committed their offenses while actively involved in other crimes, a sizable number of the assailants have exhibited some sort of extremism, mental illness, or state of delirium as the proximate motive."

Mitch wanted to keep quiet, but in his head, the leftover emotions of the morning class were mixing with the current topic of discussion, stirring deep sentiments within him. Interrupting Allen, Mitch blurted out, "The Department of Justice had to do a study to figure out people who are fucked in the head commit crimes and kill police officers?"

Allen wasn't fazed by the comment; he'd been here before. "I think what they're saying is mental health is more of an issue than previously thought," Allen replied as his eyes scanned the room. "Because of HIPPA, you can't actually do this but, if you ask anyone, in any doctor's office, who reads the med sheets for patients, they'll tell you that about forty percent or more of the patients are on some kind of mental health happy pill. Now there's two ways to look at that. One, a lot of folks take the easy way out when stressed by their life and get a script from their doctor to help them feel better. Or two, there are a lot of people out there that can't get to a doctor and really are messed up in the head and need some medication to balance them out."

"I think it still means the same thing," Mitch said. "On meds, off meds, need meds, whatever, the DOJ is stating the obvious: There are messed-up people out there, and more than ever the police are the ones who deal with it, and so we draw more casualties than ever. Does the government ever try to figure out why there are more mentally screwed-up people now than ever?"

"Naw," Allen said, "I don't think they want to know. But a lot of people, mostly outside of government, have studied the problem and have come to some conclusions."

Allen flashed another PowerPoint slide onto the screen. He glanced at the screen, then looked back at the class and started to recite from memory. "When I was growing up in the sixties, there were six mass shootings in the US. That's going with the definition of four or more people killed in one incident. In the seventies, there were sixteen, thirty two in the eighties, and forty-two in the nineties. In the 2000s, there were twenty-eight. An organization called Everytown for Gun Safety, citing media reports and official records, states there have been one hundred and seventy-three mass shootings in the United States between 2009 and 2017."

The room was quiet as each officer knew that every passing year increased the odds they would have to respond to an active shooter or mass-shooting incident. Allen continued: "Now, a lot of things have happened socially in the last half-century, but one of the most fundamental things is the acceptance of being a single parent. The government has gone out of its way to subsidize the single-parent household. But they haven't been able to replace having two adults raise a child. A lot of these mass shooters are socially awkward. Having two adults in the home, raising the children, demonstrating how to handle stress and rejection, might be the single biggest thing the general public can do to reduce all types of shootings. Do you guys know what the out-of-wedlock birthrate is for the different races in our country?"

No one answered. A new PowerPoint screenshot of graphs flashed on the screen as Davies took over the lecture. "I'll go back to when the Civil Rights Act was passed in 1964. At that time, the national out-of-wedlock birthrate was a mere seven percent. Now it's forty percent. For white kids, it was only two percent back then; now it's thirty percent. It's worse for blacks. In the sixties, it was twenty percent; now it's seventy-two. The government has subsidized not having a father around, and now, generations later, this is what we have: deadly black-on-black crime and a bunch of white lunatics shooting up movie theaters, schools, and churches. Throw in the influence of the Internet where rudderless souls troll websites promoting mass killings and some ISIS-wannabe nut jobs and you have the whole package."

The officers in the class sat in silence, digesting what was being presented to them. For most of the senior officers, they were being presented facts they knew almost anecdotally. They had been on the job long enough to see toddlers grow to become just like their mothers and absentee fathers were, useless and sometimes violent. The fringe kids with no home life, who had found camaraderie in street gangs in the past, now found belonging in Internet chat groups where bragging about being the next mass killer would bring them what they always wanted, a moment in the spotlight just once before dying. Davies and Allen could see their students sitting a little straighter in their seats. No one was checking a cell phone.

Davies continued, "The whole idea was to have a country where no one was poor, everyone had opportunities and people could overcome prejudice. These are noble causes that no one would argue with. But in the application of those ideals, we've developed a society of single-parent homes where about twenty percent live in poverty compared to about two percent in two-parent homes. In 2003, the Centers for Disease Control did a study showing behavioral problems and psychological issues were less prevalent in two-parent homes. With the government and society's approval, being a single parent was not only acceptable but encouraged and subsidized. It was a new freedom, but no one asked the unborn children if they wanted to be brought up in a single-parent household."

Davies looked down at the table in front of him, picked up a newspaper, and said, "This is one of your local papers, yesterday afternoon's edition. According to an op-ed in it, eighty percent of Hartford's children are born fatherless. Those are the kids shooting each other. Since your town mirrors Hartford in a lot of ways, you can expect similar problems."

Allen cleared his throat and said, "So we have all these issues, and I agree that many of them come down to the breakdown of the traditional family. So, who deals with it? You do, the cops—the first responder who is always on call and just a short distance away. You get one hundred mundane calls, and then that one call of extreme violence and you have to act. And your actions have to be right. There are no mulligans. And even when you do act right, maybe saving your own life or that of another, what happens?"

"You're scrutinized," came an answer.

"By who?" Davies asked.

"Internal affairs, the administration, sometimes other cops, the media," several officers answered.

"The media," Davies exhaled. "August 2014, Ferguson, Missouri, the Michael Brown case. The officer who shot him, Darren Wilson, was portrayed in the media as a killer who shot an unarmed teenager. Even today, newspapers will cite the falsehood that Brown had his hands in the air and was surrendering when he was shot. None of the witnesses who said Brown had his hands in the air were found to be credible. The St. Louis County grand jury didn't indict

Wilson, and the Department of Justice cleared him of any civil rights violations. But the press continues to refer to the incident as 'police shoot unarmed black teenager,' not 'officer shoots assailant in self-defense.'"

"It doesn't even have to be the cops," said one officer. "I had a case a couple of weeks ago where a white woman struck a ten-year-old black child who ran into the street in front of her car. It was the kid's fault—he jumped into the street out of nowhere—and she stopped about two car lengths from where she hit the kid. I get there almost immediately, and I see all the neighborhood thugs jumping on and around the lady's car. She's terrified. More cops get there, and the hoodlums retreat to their porches to continue drinking their forties. But here's the best part: Even the thugs who actually witnessed the accident gave statements that the kid ran out in front of the car with no warning, far from any crosswalk. And we even found a couple who said she stopped right away. But when the media—both TV and print—got there, every one of those hoods came out and said it was the woman's fault, that she tried to flee the scene, and they were heroes for stopping her. The accident investigation is complete, the kid is okay, but we don't see any reporters coming around for a follow-up."

"That's because if they did," Mitch interjected, "they would have to put into print, 'We screwed up and got the story wrong.'"

"I agree with you," Allen said. "It seems journalism has gone from reporting the news to inciting controversy. 'If it bleeds, it leads,' you might say. Topics such as white-versus-black or cops-versus-citizens are a reporter's dream. They get the headline out there with just enough facts to suck in the viewers and keep them excited or angry. So you, the cops doing your job, develop this attitude toward the press, your administration, IA, or the public in general. How does it affect how you do your jobs?"

"If you sit in your cruiser and do crossword puzzles

instead of getting out to check on suspicious or nefarious acts," came one answer, "you're less likely to be the next face of law enforcement for social media to piss on."

"You could get an inside job and avoid the whole problem," came another.

"Let the citizens fight it out amongst themselves. We'll pick up the pieces when they're done," was another comment.

"That's the Ferguson Effect," said Allen. "That's what some are calling it, when you guys back off from proactive policing because of the demoralizing effect of unbalanced media coverage, politicians overeager to crucify officers before due process is complete, or lack of backing from department leaders. The resulting effect of reduced proactive policing is higher crime rates. Depending on which statistics you look at, there has been anywhere from an eleven to sixteen percent increase in homicides in 2015 in twenty-five of the thirty largest cities in the country since Ferguson. Across the country, cops are definitely dialing it back."

"The whole thing is ridiculous," Mitch started again. "My guys have to hand out a card stating the steps a motorist can take if they want to make a complaint about how the officer conducted themselves during the car stop. The very idea of law enforcement is that we're the authority who administers the laws enacted by the people we're supposed to serve. By handing out complaint cards, we're basically telling the citizens to be in charge of the enforcement action, you know—I write you a ticket, you write me a ticket—it undermines our authority. So, if my guys don't stop cars, they don't get an inbox full of complaints."

"We get paid the same whether we're writing tickets or playing 'Words with Friends' on our cell phones," another voice summed up.

"Who suffers when no one stops cars for violations or gets out of their cruiser to check on suspicious acts?" Davies asked. After a long pause, he answered his own question:

"Obviously, it's the citizens that you are ideally supposed to protect and serve."

Lenny, a veteran officer, piped up. "Ideals go out the window shortly after a hundred and thirty-five pound thirteen-year-old girl kicks you in the balls and calls you a motherfucker. That's after she kicked the shit out of two other kids in the neighborhood. *Ideally*, she wouldn't have been punched and kicked to the ground and roughly handcuffed by the arresting officer, and *ideally,* some of that rough handcuffing part wouldn't have been caught by a video phone. *Ideally*, the officer should have shown restraint despite the fact that his nuts are occupying the same space as his eyeballs. *Ideally,* I would not have been the officer in that video."

"You're just pissed that you lost a fight to a thirteen-year-old," chimed in one of the other officers.

Lenny responded with a slight smile. "The worst part was when I went home and told my wife what happened—that she's off the hook for date night that evening—she goes, *woo-hoo!* and polishes off a bottle of wine by herself." Lenny then turned around to face his colleagues. "That's normal when your wife doesn't want to have sex with you, right?"

Among the chuckling, someone said, "Sure, it is."

To end the class on a high note, Allen pulled out a statistic from Ray Kelly's book, *Vigilance.* "In January 2013, when the stop and frisk debate was really heating up in New York City, the department had a seventy percent approval rating, according to the widely respected Quinnipiac University Polling Institute." Allen looked up at the class. "NYPD had been doing stop and frisk for years by that point, and a majority of the citizens believed the actions of the police department were correct and appreciated. You *are* appreciated when you do your job right, no matter what the core of that other thirty percent may say or do. When you're having a bad day, just know most people couldn't do your job. There will always be a love/hate relationship with policing. If you're here for the love, you're going to be disappointed. If you can't tolerate the hate, you're in for a long, hard career."

"And if you're in it for the humor, just follow Lenny around as he interacts with teenagers," said one of Lenny's mates.

The class was over. Special Agent Allen and Chief Davies were making small talk with some of the officers, handing out business cards. Mitch's mood had soured during the class. Walking past Paul's office, Mitch stuck his head in and said, "I'm heading over to the Last Precinct if you want to join me."

Paul took the invite as a hint that something was on Mitch's mind. "I'll be there in ten minutes or so."

15

Monday
July 24
1400 hours

As Mitch and Paul were making their way to the Last Precinct, Donna sat in the driver's seat of her patrol car in the rear lot of the PD. She was watching Gerald listen to Sergeant Fletcher, the vice, intelligence, narcotics squad supervisor. A few minutes earlier, over the radio, they and two other patrol units were ordered to meet Fletcher at the station ASAP but weren't told why. Now Donna watched as officers dressed in black battle dress uniforms, BDUs, with their faces covered by balaclavas, were loading a battering ram and what appeared to be long pry bars into a black van. Some of the BDU-clad cops held rifles like what she had seen in war movies. Half the officers dressed in black had Hartford Police Department stenciled across their shirts. The other half had North Hayward.

Gerald turned from Fletcher and quickly walked back to the cruiser while folding a white sheet of paper in half. "I have to drive," he said to Donna as he opened the driver's side door, "We're going to assist on a drug raid." Donna quickly got out and settled into the passenger's seat. Gerald handed Donna the sheet of paper he had been folding and put the cruiser in gear.

Gerald was talking fast and in a clipped way as he spoke to Donna. "Hartford PD has a search warrant for drugs at 16 Rosemary Street, which is a dead end. It will be the last house on the right as we pull in. The guy they are targeting is pictured on that sheet I just gave you." Gerald drove out of the parking lot, following the van and two dark blue police Crown Victorias. "The guy in that picture is a Dominican, passes himself off as a Puerto Rican, and should be considered armed and dangerous. The narc officers will be going into the house. Our job, along with the other two patrol units, will be to maintain an outside perimeter. Our responsibility is simple but important. Anybody who isn't a cop that leaves the target house can't get past us."

Donna studied the photo in her hands and tried to picture how the raid would unfold as the small caravan turned onto Rosemary Street. She could have never imagined what would happen next.

"Be quiet, keep the volume on your radio down and stay right next to me," were Gerald's instructions as they exited their cruiser. Gerald and Donna slow-jogged in the direction they had parked, keeping parked cars between them and the target house, turning right onto a short driveway of an adjacent property lot. They squeezed between the old hulk of a Kia with flat tires and a weathered metal shed, using the Kia as cover. Gerald squatted by the car's front fender and placed his right hand on the grip of his holstered gun. Donna assumed the same posture by the trunk. "Eyes on the house, watch the windows," Gerald said.

Donna's eyes reflexively caught and stared at the movement of the raid team as they silently stacked up in a tight single file by the front door of the three-story house. A moment later, she heard the raid team yelling, "Police!" and the simultaneous crack of the front doorjamb being splintered by the battering ram. In one fluid motion, the entry team went in.

There was movement outside the house.

As her eyes turned back to the windows, she caught sight of a body falling, arms wildly swinging and feet fluttering in short, choppy kicks. The body hit the ground with a thud/ crack that Donna could hear from forty feet away.

"Holy shit!" Gerald said as he half tripped, rounding the front of the Kia, sprinting toward the person who had just jumped out a small third-story window of the target house, unholstering his gun as he ran. Donna followed behind him, squeezing her gun between both hands in front of her, racing to keep up.

"Cover me while I handcuff him," Gerald said as they approached the nude body. Donna kept her gun pointed at the naked man who, lying on his belly with his underwear around his ankles, was struggling to crawl away as Gerald stood over him.

"He's the target," Gerald said as he clicked the handcuffs onto the belly crawler's wrists. Donna now recognized the face at her feet as the one pictured and began to relax a bit. "We're exposed here, and the entry team hasn't finished clearing the house, so stay alert," Gerald said.

Donna nodded her understanding, gazed up, and began to scan the windows again while backing up to a corner of the house. She could hear loud voices from inside the house begin yelling, "Clear!" as they swept each room for any dangers. After a couple of minutes, Fletcher came outside the front door shouting, "All clear."

Gerald called out to Fletcher, "Come around the corner, Sarge. We got something for you."

"This our Dominican?" Fletcher asked.

"I believe he is," said Gerald, "But I thought he was Puerto Rican."

"Either way, he's a piece of drug-dealing shit. I'll call for an ambulance. . . . And take the cuffs off. I don't think he's going anywhere."

With a Spanish accent, the Dominican cried, "Help me, you fuckers! This is your fault." He was rolling back and forth on his belly in pain. Pressing his forehead into the asphalt of the driveway, he screamed, "My fucking legs are broke, and I'm a fucking Puerto Rican!"

The good news, that a drug dealer was seriously fucked up outside on the driveway, spread fast. All the raid team cops took an impromptu break from their duties to gather around their wanted man. The questions and answers began to flow between them.

"Where'd he come from?"

"He jumped out the third-floor window."

"With his underwear around his ankles?"

"Yup, I got to the top floor first, just in time to see his feet disappear out that window," a Hartford officer said, "There's still a turd floating in the toilet."

Fletcher spoke up, "Based on the facts and circumstances presented, we would have to conclude that Mr. Shithead drug dealer here was on the throne, panicked, and jumped out the window when the police came knocking."

"Good times," Gerald flatly stated.

Through a long, loud, gut-emanating groan, the Dominican grunted through clenched teeth, "Fuck you. You have to help me, motherfuckers."

Fletcher shrugged his shoulders, "Ambulance is on the way, asshole." Turning to Gerald, he said, "You two watch him while everyone else goes about their duties."

Fletcher looked at Donna for a second then back at Gerald with a hard look. Gerald picked up on the meaning of Fletcher's glare: *Is this new chick, Donna, going to be a problem with what they have said to or how they have treated the Dominican?*

Donna stepped closer to Gerald as Fletcher walked away. The sound of an ambulance siren a few blocks away was getting louder. "Should we be doing something for him?" she asked.

Gerald said, "Well, we aren't doctors or even EMTs. Our first aid kit in the cruiser is the size of a cigar box, and it's full of Band-Aids, which aren't going to help our friend here.

So no, we're not going to do something for him." Donna gave a slight nod then watched as the ambulance pulled up to the curb.

Ten minutes later, Donna was back in the driver's seat of the cruiser as they pulled away from 16 Rosemary Street. The Dominican had been loaded into the ambulance and handcuffed to the gurney with a patrol officer guarding him while the narc guys methodically searched the house for any more contraband. Sergeant Fletcher had talked to Gerald privately for a few moments before he returned to their cruiser.

Gerald turned to Donna as she drove and said, "Good times! They're finding drugs in the house, plus one gun, and one drug dealer, an illegal immigrant Dominican, is seriously fucked up and going to jail. Success all the way around."

Donna nodded, and after a moment said, "A lot happened all at once, very fast, then it was back to normal speed."

"Yes, things do happen very fast and then stop or slow down." Gerald paused and said, "To get back to your question about helping the Dominican while he was writhing in pain on the ground, I get your question. Even though he was a shithead drug dealer peddling poison to the addicted, he was in an enormous amount of pain, and it can be hard to watch up close, but you have to mentally triage the moment. Do you know what I mean?"

Donna didn't react, so Gerald continued. "It's like a flow chart in your head. 'What's the most urgent problem in front of me?' is the first question. The next questions are, 'What can I do? What should I do? What have I been trained to do? What am I equipped to do? What is safe to do? and Will an action on my part make the situation better or worse?' If the answer is yes to the questions, then you take action. If not, wait and re-assess." Gerald could see Donna nodding and continued. "In this case, it was still an active scene when he jumped. We didn't know what else was going to happen. I couldn't even be sure of what window he came out of. We didn't know who he was at first, and I seriously thought he was going to get up and run. Mental triage time. . . . We secured him with handcuffs and backed ourselves up to some kind of cover. A few minutes later, the scene was secure, and the shithead is crying in pain. Nothing we could do that would ease his pain but wait for the ambulance. There were no yeses in the triage flow chart for that moment."

"I get it," Donna said. "It was just a little weird standing around while he cried in pain, even if he is a shithead."

"You'll have to get used to it," Gerald said. "You'll see shitheads, victims, and innocents get pretty fucked up on this job. It's all part of the show."

A smile crept across Donna's face. "I'll have to admit, that was a pretty good show."

16

Monday
July 24
1530 hours

TRAINING NCO PAUL WALSH WALKED the two blocks to the Last Precinct. Mitch was already there, sitting on a barstool, one empty bottle in front of him, and half of a second beer gone when Paul walked in. "Didn't care for the class?" Paul asked.

"People forget," Mitch said in response. Paul stood behind the bar, cracking open a beer and putting a ten on the bar top. It would cover both of Mitch's beers and one more for himself.

"You lost me," Paul finally said.

"Cops are killed for wearing their uniform—for doing their job. You know twelve cops were killed in the line of duty in the first nine weeks of 2016? I don't see the Department of Justice, or any other law enforcement institution, getting in front of the press and stating, 'You kill a cop and we're coming after you, your family, and everything you've ever held dear. We'll put you in jail, and we will execute you.' But a cop kills someone, and it's the DOJ, POTUS, the press, and every other jackass in the world fucking with your life. Even after it's proven to be a good shoot, like in Ferguson or even nearby in Hartford, a cop has lost his home, his job, his name is shit, and he'll have no money left. But worse,

I don't think anyone outside of our job knows how much it hurts when we lose someone."

Mitch finished his second beer and motioned for Paul to open another. "You weren't here when Brad was killed, right?" Mitch asked.

"Happened two years before I was hired."

"Want to hear the whole story?"

Paul had heard several versions of Officer Bradford Atwood's murder over the years from other officers, most of whom didn't have direct knowledge of the case. Mitch had never opened up about it until now.

"Sure." Paul put a twenty on top of the ten.

Mitch was quiet for a moment, taking a pull from his Budweiser. "I imagine it was over in an instant. I mean, when you're shot in the head, do you hear anything, feel anything? I don't know. I wasn't there when he was killed, but this is what happened—at least what I *think* happened. And any asshole who assumes it won't happen to them because he thinks he's a better cop is truly an asshole because Brad had his shit together.

"A call comes in to dispatch, and a nervous voice tells the dispatcher there's an officer down in the hallway. The dispatcher wants the caller to go out there and see what's going on, if the officer's hurt. The caller's like, 'No way. I'm not going out there.' The caller says he heard a noise, someone saying stop, and a loud bang. He peeks out of the apartment door and sees the cop on the floor. What the caller didn't know—and neither did the dispatcher—was that a few seconds earlier, Brad had interrupted the end of an active home invasion."

Paul sat motionless, taking in each word. Mitch spoke. "Let me back up a second. You see, Brad had been sent to check on a noise complaint—we all know that kind of call in an apartment building is usually bullshit, right? It's a stereo up too high, or a loud conversation, or the neighbors are stomping on their floor above, or it's a neighbor's kid who

159

won't stop crying." Paul nodded slightly as Mitch continued. "So Brad was sent on a noise complaint to the second floor of the apartment building, gets to the end of the hall, and sees two people, a guy and a chick, leaving an apartment. He tells them to stop, but they keep on walking away toward the other end of the hall. Brad senses something's wrong and catches up to them—it's a short hallway—and puts his hand on the guy's shoulder. The guy spins around and has a small revolver in his hand that Brad doesn't see or know about. He faces Brad—Brad probably thought he was going to take a punch to the head. And Brad was a tough fucker, so some skinny, candy-ass shit, which was what this guy was, couldn't possibly throw a punch to take Brad down. But this candy-ass wasn't throwing a punch. He puts that revolver to Brad's forehead and pulls the trigger. That's when the neighbor calls up and tells the dispatcher about the cop down in the hallway.

"Now dispatch, after hearing about the officer down, can't raise Brad on the radio, so the call goes out: Officer down."

Mitch took a deep breath and another pull from his beer. "When bad things happen, if you're lucky, you have someone who has their shit together to show up. The street sergeant that night was Gary Callahan, since retired. He was one of the original ERT members, with years of experience behind him from patrol and detective work, and it was a fucking good thing he was working. He arrives with two other officers and finds Brad. I don't have to go into the details of what that looked like, but it was an *oh fuck* scene. Not just because they're looking at one of their guys seriously fucked up, but Callahan also was thinking, *Who did this? Are we in their sights right now? Are they about to shoot one of us? I've got a crime scene to protect.*—There's a million questions to ask dozens of residents in this building and neighborhood, and they have set up a perimeter. He had observed two people running down the street away from this building as he was pulling up—are they the suspects? And they have to get Brad to the fucking hospital. Callahan handled all of that. He's got one side of his head thinking tactics and the other side thinking crime scene with the overall thought of finding who did this quickly, and he knows there aren't enough cops on his squad to do it all. Callahan and his guys did it. They kept their shit together.

"The call for mutual aid went out along with a page to all ERT members, which, back then, I'd just joined. At the time, we all had pagers—this is before cell phones were common, so I get the page: *Officer shot. Report to scene.* It doesn't say who or how bad or if they're alive. My wife and I were having dinner with friends in Simsbury when I got the page. We quickly said goodnight to our friends and got into our old Toyota. I told my wife, 'We're not stopping for any red lights or stop signs. Your job is to look to the right for any traffic when we come to an intersection and tell me if anyone's coming.' Well, what was normally a twenty-five-minute trip from the center of Simsbury to headquarters took twelve, and that Toyota has been making a weird noise ever since. I hop out of the car at headquarters and tell my wife to call my parents and let them know it's not me who was shot."

Mitch sighed. "I grab my gear and find a ride to the scene. Not easy, as every fucking vehicle the PD has was in use, but I finally get a ride. When I get there, and this is maybe thirty to forty minutes after Brad had been shot, there's a hundred cops there. State cops, local cops, I saw cruisers from towns forty miles away, and more were arriving code three, lights and sirens. And Hartford PD, I'll tell you those guys are the best . . ." a wave of emotion suddenly came over Mitch. "Those guys had every intersection in Hartford between the town line and the hospital blocked off, so the medical unit carrying Brad had a straight shot to the emergency room.

"So I get there and step into the command trailer, and our chief at the time is an old mick—I can smell the wine on his breath ten feet away—and he's conferring with a chief from another town, who also has wine on his breath. I'm thinking, *At least brush your teeth, assholes,* but they just talked in circles, back and forth like it's the first time they've handled a case, and they're not making any decisions. Again, Callahan did a great job in the heat of the moment, and these assholes, who call themselves chiefs, are just fucking things up forty-five minutes later while the scene gets colder by the second.

"Sometime in the middle of the night, we get word that the motherfucker we're looking for is holed up nearby in an empty house. It was probably just speculation on someone's part. You know how it goes: An investigator finds out the house is empty and, given its proximity to the crime scene, speculates the bad guy is hiding in it. Word gets out, and it almost becomes de facto that the bad guy is in this empty house, so the ERT is loaded into a van, and we speed down the street with the intention of us sweeping the place and either catching or killing the fucker.

"Now Declan Harmon is always the first officer through the door in any ERT training or actual raid—he's got a custom shotgun—and I'm always next with my automatic rifle. I'm figuring we're going to get there and line up at the door the way we always do, and Declan and I are going through, one and two like always, with the rest of the team following. And I'm thinking we're going into a house with a cop killer inside and he has nothing to lose by shooting Declan, me, or anyone else on the team, and my pucker factor goes through the roof. And I also know, at that moment, I'll have no problem pulling my trigger and killing the fucker, and my biggest fear is to not make a mistake that gets someone on the team hurt, which translates into being quick and accurate on the trigger. Just don't fuck up."

Mitch shook his head. "The van pulls over, and the team leader is chatting on his radio. Turns out someone was using their head—several patrol officers surrounded the empty house before we got there and sent in a K9 to sweep it for any people. The dog didn't find anyone; the house was empty.

"No one in the van says a thing as it turns around to go back to the command post. But you know, every single one of us was thinking the same thing: A minute earlier, we were very likely heading face-first into a shootout, and no one hesitated to get into the van. No one backed down.

"Dawn breaks and most of us have been up twenty-four hours or more by now. I know less than nothing about what had happened the night before, and people who were in charge didn't know much more. Still, investigators were able to piece together that there was a home invasion in which an older Hispanic guy was badly beaten at the same time Brad was shot, and Callahan had observed two people running away past the soda bottling factory toward the river when he arrived on scene. It's decided we need to sweep the fields and swamp behind the factory down to the river's edge. The chance of a suspect being there in the swamp, hiding for twelve hours—remember, it's January, and a cold rain had been falling all night—was small. But we had to do it. One, just to be thorough, two, to try and find any evidence, and three, maybe the motherfucker *is* still out there, which was very motivating."

Mitch picked up his almost-empty bottle, studying it a moment before finishing it off. Paul slipped behind the bar and popped the cap on another, setting it in front of his fellow sergeant. "Anyway, during the night, several other SWAT and ERT teams from other towns started showing up—maybe sixty, seventy guys in all. Now it's morning, and we all line up, shoulder to shoulder behind the factory, seventy heavily armed cops in the cold, wet air, and we step off in unison into the field and swamp. The frozen brown grass crunched under our feet and boots filled up with cold water as we marched to the edge of Route 2. It was kind of eerie that no one was talking. The only voices were squad leaders giving the occasional command to stay in line and watch our spacing. Or an expletive when someone sank up to their knees in the water. We get to Route 2 and wait for some state troopers to shut down the highway. Before they do, citizens are driving by, gawking at us, probably not knowing why we're by the guardrail, carrying long guns, and not looking happy. The troopers close the highway, and we cross, get to the river's edge and wheel around and reverse direction, covering the other half of the swamp back to the area of the soda bottling factory.

"The rest of the day for me and the other guys of the ERT was spent in standby mode. Some of the guys shed their armor and secured their long guns and went to work investigating. The folks in the factory let us use their cafeteria to dry off and stay warm. Sometime during the morning Lieutenant Beal, who headed both the ERT and detective bureau at the time, called the team together in a corner of the cafeteria, and he announced that Brad was dead. We all kind of knew it, hearing a few whispers here and there during the night, but to have it spoken aloud and know it's true. . . ."

Mitch gulped down the last half of his fifth beer, sat back on his barstool, and shook his head, a half-smile on his face, his unfocused eyes staring at the ceiling. "You know what's fucked up? Our police leadership didn't know *what* to do. They had no plan in place for the aftermath and investigation of a line-of-duty death. They just figured the state police would come in and perform the investigation, and the rest of us would pull our shifts, supply an honor guard, and go about our business. But that's not going to happen in any organization. The administrators had never been trained to handle something like this."

"Not sure what you mean," Paul said.

"Look, in the Army or US Marines, if you're a lieutenant in an infantry company, your training puts you into scenarios where, for example, you order a squad out to patrol some enemy territory, and they never come back. They're missing in action or killed in action; you don't know, but you're trained to work through it to accomplish the mission. That kind of training puts a stark reality on the idea that some of your guys died following your orders."

Paul replied, "I get part of what you're saying, that you have to train to deal with adverse conditions. But I'm not sure I see where you're going with this."

Mitch knew he was starting to ramble. The beers were having their effect as thoughts came into his head faster than he could organize them. After a concentrated pause, he started, "As cops, we see other people dying fucked-up deaths all the time, but we don't mourn those dead. We feel bad, but they're not close to us. But when we lose one of our own, we not only see the tragedy up close, but we have to *mourn and do our job.* And there's survivor's guilt for many of the guy's squadmates. They're thinking, 'It should have been me,' or, 'If I had done something different Brad wouldn't have been killed,' but there was nothing they could have done differently that would have changed the outcome. Brad was ambushed, and there isn't a cop out there that wouldn't have been caught in the same trap."

A moment of clarity came to Mitch. "It's not until after we lose one of our own that the chiefs even think about how to handle it, and they handled it wrong in Brad's case. You see, they weren't there to see Brad dying in that hallway, or hear his pager constantly going off—his family and friends were paging, desperate for a call back from him. The old mick, he was just giving out orders, but he didn't realize he was out of people to perform duties. Everybody was already working or had mentally checked out. Am I making any sense?"

"Yeah, I get it," said Paul. "Lack of leadership when you need it most."

"Fuckin' exactly," Mitch continued. "That shit-for-brains Deputy Chief Russell—remember him?"

"He died in a car wreck around six months after he retired, right?"

"That's the one."

"And no one was very upset when it happened."

"Nor should they have been, but anyway. . . . I passed by his office later that afternoon—this is maybe eighteen or twenty hours after Brad was shot—and I look in. He's sitting in his captain's chair, feet up on his desk, lobbing a baseball up in the air as he stares out his window at the stoplight at School and Tolland Street. Jackass thought the state police would just run on autopilot and conduct the investigation, and he'd just sit back and do nothing like always. Meanwhile, the troopers are looking to him to provide some basic directions, like where to set up a long-term command post, points of contact, available personnel—you know, simple command-and-control shit that anyone wearing a chief's star on their collar better be able to perform. He was just incapable."

Paul cleared the gathering empties and pulled out two more cold ones. "You started talking about how they forget. What do you mean?"

"I mean this," Mitch said, now refocused. "For years after Brad was killed, there was a memorial service at the church around the corner from the PD on the anniversary of his death. The first year, the church was packed and included some—but not all—of the administrators. Second year, there's none—no admin. And no mayor or anyone from town hall. The *never forget* slogan was a thing of the past. Robert Coughlin is our new chief by then, and he has all his idiot deputy chiefs surrounding him, and none of these guys ever did understand how much it hurt when Brad was killed. They didn't know him or understand the anxiety his death caused everyone who worked the street. They had no idea. It isn't in their DNA to understand, and it made the pain worse."

"For example?" Paul asked.

"You want an example? Here's one that shows how bad it was. Two years after Brad's death, there's a dedication ceremony in the lobby of the PD to unveil a relief portrait of Brad. Part of the ceremony is to award Anson Webber a medal for breaking the case and finding a critical lead that led us to Brad's killer. You know that part of the story?"

"Nope."

"Webber was a patrol officer in Hartford, and a couple of nights after Brad was killed, he made a routine traffic stop. Webber, being a good street cop, engages the operator of the vehicle in a conversation that comes around to inquiring about any info on who killed the North Hayward cop. Webber, again being on his game, notices a change in the operator's body language—a slight hesitation, you know, like he's nervous. Now Webber is one of the least offensive guys there is. Even when he's in uniform, people on the street talk to him easily. So the operator of the vehicle starts saying that he knows who killed Brad and provides details that no one would know. Webber up-channels the info and is told to report to the command center first thing next morning. Me and the rest of us in the field get a page and are ordered to be at the command post at 0700."

Mitch continued after a pause. "Let me backtrack a bit. After the arrests had been made and the active part of the case was winding down, I was tasked with reading every piece of paper generated by the case and putting it all in order. So, I know, based on confessions and statements from Tanneros and his co-conspirators and witnesses, how this whole thing started. You see, the asshole who killed Brad, Alejandro Tanneros, had a lot on his mind two days after committing the murder. What had seemed to be an easy plan to get a few thousand dollars went really bad. It was so simple when he'd come up with the idea. This chick named Alexia had become friends with an old man who kept his money in his apartment. The old man liked to brag to the pretty twenty-two-year-old that he had thousands of dollars, and he'd take care of her if she would just take care of him. 'You don't have to marry me,' the old man would say, 'just keep me company in my old age.' Alexia would just smile and get him his Crown Royal and give him a peck on the forehead. Alexia was pregnant and needed the money she made taking care of the old man three days a week. But there was no way she was going to live with him. If she could just *find* the thousands of dollars he kept bragging about, she could take it and run. But she also knew the cops would be looking for her if the money went missing. As far as she could tell, she was the only person to come visit the old man. If the money disappeared and she stopped showing up, it would be an easy case for the cops, and she'd be having her baby in prison.

"So she confided to her cousin, Serena, about the old man and the money. Serena listened and casually said she would talk to her boyfriend, Tanneros. 'He knows about these things,' Serena said. 'He's been to jail and shit, so he would know how to rob a guy.'

"Tanneros, indeed, had been to jail and shit, but really didn't know about these things, because he kept on being sent back to jail. 'Hey baby,' Serena tells Tanneros, 'you remember my little cousin, Alexia? She knows where some money at. She say something like thousands in this old guy's apartment. She pregnant and shit, so she thinkin' you could help her get the money an' she wouldn't hafta work no more.' Tanneros said he'd come up with a plan."

Mitch frowned. "Three days later, Tanneros and Serena, along with Alexia, were parked in a beat-up Taurus outside the complex. 'All's you gots to do,' Tanneros says, 'is get us into the building and show us the apartment. Then you leave and waits here in the car.' Alexia thought it was the perfect plan. Tanneros and Serena would knock on the old man's door, get inside the apartment, and steal his money. In five minutes, she'd be rich, even after splitting the money with Tanneros and Serena.

"According to Alexia's statement, she waited five minutes, then ten. Then a cop showed up. Alexia started her car, driving back home. She was about a mile away, crossing the Charter Oak Bridge, when she heard sirens—lots of them."

Mitch pushed himself away from the bar and stood as he continued his narrative. "You and I both know penitentiaries are the higher learning centers for the career criminal. Each additional incarceration, from juvenile detention to a max security prison, is a merit badge for some and a solid learning experience for most. Some learn from the experience and become better criminals, some don't. Tanneros fell into the latter category.

"It was also to his disadvantage that he was not all that strong physically. So, when the old man opened the door, and Tanneros pushed him back into the apartment, the old man gave him a punch to the solar plexus that left him doubled over. Serena went into combative-bitch mode, a mode she later said she learned keeping her lecherous uncles and cousins out of her pants once she hit puberty. That's also why she dated Tanneros; she knew she could take him in a fight. Serena kicked the old man in the balls, taking him down to the floor, and then she grabbed a half-empty Crown Royal bottle off the TV stand and smashed it over the old man's head, knocking him unconscious. 'I had him 'til he sucker-punched me, motherfucker,' groaned Tanneros. 'Let's tie him up and find the money.' Using an extension cord, they tied the unconscious man's hands and feet and rummaged around the apartment looking for the cash.

"It didn't take long for them to find the safe in the bottom of the bedroom closet—or the loaded revolver sitting on top of it. But after that, Tanneros' plan fell apart. Of course, it wasn't his fault he got punched in the gut and made an awful lot of noise, and it wasn't his fault the old man was unconscious, making it impossible to get the combination to the safe. Whenever he gets caught, nothing's ever *his* fault. And he was determined not to get caught—or go back to jail—this time. He was going to get the money, quit that job at the car wash, and live a good life. He would make this plan work.

"Tanneros and Serena began to kick the old man as he

lay on the floor, yelling at him to wake up and tell them the combination. They were in stupid-criminal mode now, neither of them thinking how absurd it was to try to beat an unconscious man into consciousness." Mitch wore a sneer of contempt.

"They tried to lift the safe, but it was too heavy. Instead, they took his keys and gun, figuring they could come back at another time and finish the job when the old man wasn't home.

"Serena walked into the hallway first, with Tanneros right behind her. Just then, a cop entered the hall from the front stairwell. Neither was really looking at the tall officer approaching them. 'Hey,' the officer said, grabbing Tanneros by the left shoulder. Tanneros spun to his left, the old man's revolver in his right hand, and as the gun was about to touch the officer's head, he squeezed the trigger, turned, and walked out the back door of the building. 'I ain't going back to jail,' Tanneros said as he and Serena walked through a small housing project."

Paul took a small sip from his beer. Mitch's eyes were unfocused, staring at the wall behind the bar.

"Fast forward a couple of years to the dedication ceremony I was talking about, in honor of Brad. Chief Coughlin arrives for the ceremony. He doesn't know who Webber is. I mean, he didn't recognize his name or his face, and he was standing right next to him. So, after he mumbles through reading Webber's citation, he looks around for Webber, who politely stood there as embarrassed members of our PD quickly point out where he's standing. You see, Chief Coughlin was just going through the motions—he didn't care about Webber or any of us or our feelings. If he did, he would've been prepared. Never mind *never forget*. How about give just a little remembrance, some consolation to the family, a pat on the back to the people who worked the case? But no, outreach and understanding weren't part of his personal agenda, and there's a bunch of assholes in this PD now following his lead. Coughlin is just another example of poor leaders who are self-serving assholes. They forget about the past or what's important. They really don't care."

Paul finished his beer, then looked at Mitch, raising an eyebrow while tipping the beer bottle in Mitch's direction. Mitch nodded, and Paul grabbed two more from the cooler.

Mitch continued. "You know Lieutenant Steve Medioli in Hartford?"

"No," Paul answered.

"I've worked with him on a few cases. He's good. Anyway, he was working as the street sergeant in Hartford during this investigation when he got a call from some of the troopers working Brad's case. The troopers tell Medioli they have good information that Tanneros is holed up in his aunt's home, a second-floor apartment on Russ Street. The troopers ask Medioli for some intelligence on the layout of the apartments and neighborhood there. After comparing notes for a few minutes, Medioli and the troopers, along with some heavily armed Hartford street cops, decide to strike while the iron is hot and go knocking on the apartment door. The aunt opens up, sees all the cops, and just backs up a couple of steps to her kitchen table while gazing at the floor—total submission. The cops walk in, splitting up to search each room. As luck would have it, Medioli finds himself at a doorway, staring into a dark bedroom. He shines his light on the bed. The other cops are checking the other few rooms of the apartment. Medioli barks out, 'Come on out, Tanneros, I know you're in here.' Medioli didn't know for *sure* he was in there, so he was a little surprised to see a pair of hands come out from under the bed. Jackpot! He's got a cop killer cornered, just five feet away—he could shoot him, end this right now. His finger moves off the trigger guard and onto the trigger, waiting for Tanneros to make a sudden move, anything to justify shooting him. He slowly crawls out. Medioli has his gun sights literally on Tanneros' head when another cop comes up from behind. Tanneros is moving slowly, obeying

171

the cop's commands. Medioli's finger comes off the trigger. Tanneros doesn't resist and is easily handcuffed and taken to Hartford PD.

"Hours later, in one of the interview rooms at the Hartford PD major crimes office, the detectives were finally done talking to him. There was enough evidence to formally charge him, and word was sent back to the command post for North Hayward police officers to come and get him. A half-hour later, Sergeant Callahan and two of Brad's squadmates arrive in the office.

"Now, I witnessed this part myself. Their uniforms are crisp. They're almost marching when they walk in. The entire office, which takes up half of the second floor of the building, is full of North Hayward officers. They're victims of the crime too, and in mourning. Nods are exchanged, and the interview room door opens. Tanneros steps out, his eyes to the floor, hands cuffed behind his back. Callahan wants the cuffs removed, and a detective standing behind Tanneros takes them off. The only sound is the clicking from the ratchet in the cuffs. Callahan looks at Tanneros, and in a clear and commanding voice, tells him to turn around and keep his hands behind his back. Tanneros does so without looking up. Callahan produces a pair of handcuffs, holds them up momentarily, and announces, 'These are Brad Atwood's handcuffs, and they're going on Alejandro Tanneros while we take him to jail.' I could feel the tears in my eyes start. A voice in the room asked, 'What's he being charged with?' and Callahan responded, 'He's being charged with the murder of Officer Bradford Atwood.' The only sounds you could hear were the cuffs being clicked around Tanneros' wrists and people sniffling, trying not to cry, but we all were. Including me."

Mitch blinked away his tears, as he had many years ago, while he paused and came back to the present. "You know, I think I might've said Tanneros was a career criminal. He'd been locked up a number of times, but now, in our state, the government has started the *second chance society*, basically giving locked-up criminals a second chance to integrate into society. But the governor and the rest of the politicians who run the show bear no responsibility when it goes wrong, and the second-chancers commit more crimes. You know the governor's son committed an armed robbery back in 2009? He tried to rob a drug dealer at gunpoint. The governor said his son, who was twenty-one at the time, had emotional issues. Like that's a fucking defense. But these are the assholes that get elected."

Paul grunted, shaking his head.

"There was an effort back in 2000 by some politicians and police chiefs to make the death penalty automatic for anyone convicted of killing an on-duty police officer. The state Supreme Court squashed that effort," said Mitch.

"Why did they squash it?" asked Paul.

"The case they used for their ruling was the Trooper Bagshaw murder. Bagshaw interrupted two assholes, the Johnson brothers, in the middle of burglarizing a sporting goods store. Before Bagshaw could get out of his cruiser, Terry Johnson unloaded a fusillade of bullets into him. It's estimated Bagshaw lived fifteen to ninety seconds. The court's majority opinion was that Bagshaw didn't suffer extreme pain before he died, and that it wasn't torture."

"You're fucking kidding me."

"No joke. I've seen, you've seen, people die on this job—you know, citizens. One time I rolled up on a crowd in the middle of the street surrounding a guy lying on his back. He'd just been stabbed in the chest. He was alive, still breathing. I got on my knees, looked into his eyes, asked him who did this. He couldn't answer. He stopped breathing moments later. His heart had been sliced when he was stabbed. The guy who killed him had been convicted of other crimes where he had been present, as in *involved*, in three other slayings. Think it was torture for the stabbing victim? He *knew* he was dying. Isn't that torture enough? How about car crash victims? The moment of terror just before impact. Anyone on this job long enough has seen that a few times. Moments of terror before dying. Sounds like torture to me. But unlike a car crash, which is usually accidental, shooting someone—shooting a cop—is intentional. Cop killers want the policeman to suffer a painful death, and they want the survivors to suffer, too.

"The Johnson brothers, Tanneros, Richard Reynolds—all cop killers—they should go through the same feelings, live the same moments of despair, the anguish. There's nothing else that can equate the feelings of a person just before a violent death at the hands of a murderer. The only justice is to kill the murderers. They shouldn't get a warning. It should be that one day they wake up and are led away and shot."

"Some people deserve to die. The liberals and pacifists will never get that," said Paul.

Mitch drained the last of his beer and threw the empty bottle at the trash can behind the bar. It bounced off the rim and clanged to the floor, not breaking. Mitch let out a long sigh, "I should probably get going."

Paul nodded in agreement, finishing his beer, then picked up Mitch's empty off the floor.

"See you tomorrow, Sarge," Paul said.

"See you tomorrow."

17

Wednesday
July 26
1610 hours

GERALD STOOD IN THE WATCH commander's office, across the large desk from Lieutenant Cantu. Sergeant Onslow, the desk sergeant, knowing what the ensuing conversation was going to be about, had rolled his chair to a neutral corner.

At the start of the shift, Lieutenant Cantu had made a rare appearance in front of his squad. Standing in the front of the lineup room and actually acting like the leader of his squad was an anomaly. Leading from behind and lazy fair leadership, versus *laissez-faire,* was his style. His daily conduct spoke for him; he didn't get involved with anything unless he absolutely had to. Standing behind the small podium, Lieutenant Cantu recited the general order regarding officer conduct while on patrol. There were many "don'ts": reading books, leaving your district without authorization from a supervisor, taking prolonged breaks, smoking cigarettes in uniform, and the list went on and on. Supervisory mini-lectures were often the result of a citizen complaining about an officer. Gerald figured some cop recently got caught napping or smoking a cigar in a cruiser or rolled up their window and drove away when one of the local gadfly's approached with an imaginary, and therefore police, problem. When Cantu had completed his recitation, he took a long look at Gerald and a quick glance at Donna. He ended by stating that he was merely reminding everyone what the rules are, and it would behoove officers to follow them. *Behoove,* Gerald hated that word.

Now, an hour later, Lieutenant Cantu had called Gerald in from the street, into a closed-door session in the WC's office. Gerald could feel his blood pressure rising; he had been singled out for something, and it probably wasn't good.

Cantu had a hard time keeping eye contact with Gerald as he spoke in one long run-on sentence. "I've gotten word that you are studying for the sergeant's exam while on duty, along with taking more breaks than other guys on the squad, during which you are at the copy machine making hard copies of general orders." Cantu kept his gaze on a spot on the desk.

Gerald kept a steady stare on the top of Cantu's head. "What can I say LT, I'm doing what you and everyone else has done to get ready for a promotional exam."

Cantu glanced up. "As I stated earlier, you cannot read for personal entertainment while on duty. That includes studying. If you need to make copies of the general orders, do it on your own time."

Gerald looked over at Onslow, who gave a barely perceptible shrug of his shoulders. Gerald said, "I'm guessing you have Sergeant Onslow here as an official witness to your counseling me."

"Just keeping things aboveboard, Gerald, that's all."

"You know, LT, it's hard to keep track of which rules are enforced around here and which ones aren't." Cantu remained silent, and Gerald calculated what he would say next. "Remember, we worked midnights together way back when. I was new, and you had a few years on the job. Lots of these little general orders were broken . . . by everyone on the squad."

Cantu's focus abandoned the spot on the desk, and he finally fixed his eyes on Gerald's and said, "For one, I don't know what you're talking about. For two, that was then, and this is now. You've been officially counseled." Gerald began to turn and leave but stopped himself and squared his chest to Cantu.

"You know, lieutenant, one of the little things I've picked up in my recent reading—at home—is that integrity is the most valued of the fourteen leadership traits organizations expect from everyone in a chain of command. It's commonly defined as honesty with others and, more importantly, honesty with yourself." Gerald let his words linger. He could go on and cross swords with Cantu, but he was guessing someone else was behind this. Cantu didn't take initiative on any matter, never mind something as trivial as an officer studying between calls. Pissing on him wasn't going to accomplish anything.

The veiled insult cut through Cantu's thin skin. He stood leaning on his hands over the desk. "You're on the verge of being insubordinate!"

Gerald leaned in slightly to Cantu then turned his hands, palms up, in a mock motion of submission. *Make the call, lieutenant, or dismiss me.*

"I'll be making notes on this meeting. Officer, you're dismissed."

"That's a good idea. So will I." Gerald turned and walked out the door.

He walked out the rear door to headquarters to the cruiser Donna was in. He slid into the right front seat and slammed the door. Donna, halfway through writing a report, stopped tapping the keys on the MDT. She glanced at her FTO, curious if Gerald was upset about something and even more curious if she was the something. She went back to typing her report as Gerald buckled himself in.

"As soon as you have a good spot in your report to take a break, save it and start driving," Gerald directed. Donna did as she was told and soon was pulling out onto the four-lane road in front of the public safety complex. Gerald inhaled deeply then asked Donna, "You meet with the training NCO once a week, right? You guys go over the daily observation reports, and you give him feedback on your training."

"Yeah, actually, it's been a little more than a week since I sat down with him. He was out the day we were supposed to get together."

"Okay, yeah, I remember he was out for a few days last week 'cause I was supposed to see him to schedule a qualification day for some of our remedial shooters. Um, does anyone else ask you about you riding with me? What we do during a shift?

"No, not that I can think of. Why?"

"Apparently Lieutenant Cantu is aware that while you write reports, I read up on my study material. Also, someone has noticed that while you are on your bathroom breaks, I am at the copy machine making copies of study material."

"Why would Lieutenant Cantu care? We're not missing any calls."

"It's not really your concern what goes on between me and Lieutenant Cantu. Just do me a favor and let me know if anyone seems overly inquisitive about what I am doing during a shift."

Donna began to feel the heat of guilt under her uniform as her mind wrestled with how to say what she knew without casting blame on herself.

The dispatcher's pitched voice came through the cruiser radio, assigning Donna and Gerald to a verbal domestic between two women. Donna knew the approximate location of the address. No need to have dispatch repeat the call or look at the MDT for directions. At least she was getting to know her way around town.

Driving into a housing project that consisted of elderly housing on one side and divided families on the other, Donna pulled up several car lengths away from two women yelling at each other. The word *bitch* was the most prevalent word coming from either woman's mouth. They stood in the dirt patch that was once a front yard but was now a parking spot for older, entry-level economy vehicles, one of which was operational.

Before they exited the cruiser, Gerald said, "I want you to get used to talking to citizens and inquiring at the same time. So you start talking to them, find out what the problem is, and determine if there needs to be an arrest. If you get stuck, I'll jump in."

Neither woman, both of whom appeared to be in their late twenties, seemed surprised that two police officers were approaching them. They argued right up to the moment Donna addressed them. "Good evening, ladies, what's the problem here?"

The first woman, who identified herself as Sandie (ie on the end, not y) said, "She's moving out and taking somethin' that ain't hers."

This prompted the second woman, named Sarah, to retort, "It belongs to me. I paid for it."

"Bullshit, I paid for it, and I gots the receipt."

"What item are we talking about?" Donna interjected, trying to redirect the focus of their anger.

"This," Sarah said as she pulled a large strap on purple dildo out from the top of an overstuffed backpack.

Good times. "How long have you two been living together?" Donna asked.

"'Bout two years. We were lovers," Sandie replied as she flicked away the beginning of a teardrop with her finger, quickly adding, "An' I gots a receipt for it!"

"No, you don't. I bought this, and I gots a witness!"

"Who would the witness be?" asked Donna.

"My grandmother."

"If you have a witness, then—"

In a Joe Friday voice, Gerald stepped into the conversation. "Where did you and your grandmother purchase the dildo?"

"At the Sensual Supply Shop. 'Bout two years ago."

"You and your grandmother went shopping for a strap-on dildo at the Sensual Supply Shop about two years ago . . . and she can back you up on this?" *Joe Friday never had a call like this.*

Sandie started again. "We shared that strap-on. How can you even think about taking it away!"

"I'm taking it away cuz I can't stand the thought of you using it with someone else!"

Sandie threw down her phone and shouted, "I don't care that you're leaving, but the strap-on stays here with me!"

Donna was unsure of what action she should take. A verbal dispute over property isn't a domestic by definition. Neither woman was making any threats. Her mind was leaning toward labeling this as a civil problem since no crime had or seemed likely to occur.

Gerald was talking now. Keeping his inner Joe Friday going, he explained, "Ladies, in the State of Connecticut, the strap-on dildo falls under what they call mutual property. Because you both live together and mutually used the dildo, neither one of you can claim individual ownership regardless of who paid for it." He paused a moment to let the statement sink in. "It appears both of you have a lot of sentimental emotion attached to this dildo, but one of you is going to have to give it up."

Both women stared long and hard at each other. Even the dildo didn't appear happy, hanging at a limp angle in Sarah's clenched, white-knuckled hand. Sandie bent down and picked up her phone. "Wait," she said. Sandie went inside the house for a few minutes, returning with a small gym bag that she dropped at Sarah's feet.

Sandie said, "You can have that, and I get the strap-on back." Sarah secured the dildo under her armpit and opened the gym bag, surveying its contents.

After a few moments, Sarah said, "Okay," and handed over the strap-on to Sandie without looking up. Sandie quickly strolled back into her home, as if afraid the deal might fall through if she lingered outside, and slammed her door shut.

"I assume you're leaving, and we don't have anything to worry about, like this dispute starting up again?" Gerald asked.

"No worries," Sarah replied. "My new girlfriend is coming to pick me up. Should be here any minute."

"Good. We'll just be right over there until you leave just to make sure you two don't start arguing again."

Gerald and Donna sat in their cruiser, keeping a casual eye on Sarah until her ride arrived. Once they were confident the dildo dispute was over, Donna put the cruiser in motion.

After a few minutes of silence, Gerald said, "I didn't want you to get into a conversation about witnesses or who has a right to the dildo, so I jumped in."

"I was just about to tell them it was not a police problem, that they would have to settle it themselves and keep it civil."

"That's good. It's just better to explain to citizens about mutual property, and then you can help them come to some sort of agreement."

Donna felt she had been heading toward the same conclusion without Gerald's interference. She responded with a muted, "Okay."

"Find somewhere to park where you can write up this report and the last one you were working on. You don't want to fall behind. The lieutenant runs a log every week to see who has unfinished cases. If you have too many, he starts to harangue you."

Donna said, "Speaking of the LT, I think I know how he got word of your studying and copying."

"Oh yeah, fill me in."

"The other day, before you got to lineup, a couple of the guys who get there early were joking about you moving a large binder from your personal vehicle to our cruiser. They were guessing it was the general orders book and that you study during our shift."

"Yeah, okay. Was anything else said?"

"One of then asked me if he was right and I said he was. I'm sorry if I said the wrong thing and got you in trouble."

"Don't worry about it. I'm not in trouble, and there's nothing for you to be sorry about. Just try to understand this for your own benefit: Not everyone in the department is your friend. Some, like the two clowns joking about me and my general orders book, will go out of their way to make life difficult for others just for shits and grins or for their own gain." Silently, Gerald wondered if Marty had anything to do with this. He likes to stir the pot, and judging from their conversation a week earlier, Marty is still bitter about being passed over for promotion.

Donna pulled into a vacant lot across from a small neighborhood bodega. "So you're saying guys on our own squad went to the LT to complain about you studying?"

"No, not directly. They just got the word out into the right rumor channels, which got someone higher up to put pressure on Cantu to call me in. If Cantu had any balls, he would have just dropped the matter with whoever brought it to his attention. But he's big on covering his ass. He doesn't want any potential dirt to touch him."

"I'm sorry. I just didn't know."

"You have nothing to apologize for." Gerald paused, trying to formulate the right words to say about Cantu. "You have to understand. We work with a lot of different characters here at the PD. Cantu kinda represents the professional victim. You know what I mean?"

"Not really."

"Cantu claims Native American heritage as well as Mexican heritage even though he appears as white as white can be and doesn't understand or speak a lick of Spanish."

"Just because he doesn't look Latino doesn't mean he isn't."

"I get that. Let me finish. He looks and acts like a white guy until he doesn't get what he wants. Then he becomes the double-minority Latino being discriminated against until he does get what he wants. Then he's back to being the white guy. If he was just a white guy not qualified for an assignment, then he would have to just suck it up and accept he didn't pass muster or he played the department politics wrong. But once he states that he didn't get his choice because he's of Native American or Mexican descent he's pretty much saying, 'I'm not qualified for the job, but I know you will put me in because you don't want to fight me and my minority status.'"

"Do the chiefs ever change their decision in Cantu's favor?"

"In my observations, they have caved every time to keep Cantu off their backs."

Donna, well aware of the country's actions against minorities from her college education, said, "If they change their minds, then maybe Cantu's claims are justified."

"Yeah, maybe, but let me put it another way. There's going to be a time in your career where you look at who you're working with, a squad, detective section, officers from neighboring PDs, and all you will see are hard-working, qualified people. You won't see skin color or gender or anything else. There will be other times, given the same situations, where you will work with some inept people and when the most inept of those is the one always claiming discrimination, playing the part of a professional victim. Then you can't help but see their skin color or claimed minority status and wonder if that's how they got hired or put into any given assignment."

"I'll have to take your word for it because I haven't seen or experienced what you're talking about."

Gerald tipped his head back against the headrest. The conversation had gone way past what he felt comfortable discussing with someone he didn't know too well outside the job. He took a couple of deep breaths, then smiled and said, "The great purple strap-on dildo dispute. Now that was a good times call."

18

Saturday
August 5
1005 hours

GERALD, IN GYM SHORTS AND a faded T-shirt, sat stiffly in his kitchen chair at a seated position of attention. Emily sat across the round dinette table from him, braless, her nipples pressed against her tank top. She shuffled a stack of three-by-five index cards in her hands, clunked the stack on the tabletop to level the edges, and read the question from the top card. "Name six exceptions to needing a search warrant."

Gerald responded in an almost robotic monotonous tone. "Search incident to lawful arrest, the plain view exception, consent, stop and frisk, automobile exception, and exigent circumstances." *Easy question!* He felt smug and tried not to show it. Emily's nipples looked hard. Maybe after impressing her with this mock oral promotion board, he could get a quickie.

Emily chewed her lower lip. "You have to put some inflection in your voice and turn your head to look into the eyes of each member on the panel as you answer."

"Yeah, okay. Next time."

Emily shook her head. "The oral board is less than a week away. You *have* to improve your delivery, like it's second nature!"

"This is awkward enough, having you ask me all these

test questions and pretending to be a monitor. And I'm getting horny."

Emily snatched her cell phone off the table and put it into video record mode. "When you answer the next question, I want you to look at the kitchen window, me, and the pantry door as if they are people. Now, smile, inflect your voice, and tell me, what are the critical tasks to perform in a tactical situation?"

"Establish communications, identify the kill zone, establish an inner perimeter, establish an outer perimeter, set up a command post, set up a staging area, and request resources." Gerald felt pretty good in his delivery, almost like he could be a newscaster. He had moved his head and put a little lilt in his voice.

Then Emily handed him her phone. "Play it back," she ordered. He did.

"Shit, I look like a dork and sound even worse."

Emily felt like she was coaching a client about to be put on the stand. In her attorney-trained mind, there was no excuse for lack of preparation. Gerald wasn't there yet. She wanted to encourage without haranguing. "You have to practice stating your answers. We've all been in classes where the teacher drones on and on, and whatever is being taught gets washed away in the boredom. Don't be that droning guy. You'll lose points."

"I get it. I get it."

"Last criticism. Give some depth to your answers."

"Like, what do you mean?"

"The exceptions to a search warrant question. You've probably had cases where you have used most of those exceptions. Use your experience as a guide and tell the story of how the exceptions worked."

Gerald's shoulders slumped. "I thought I had a good handle on all of this."

"You do, but so will everyone else. They're all studying the same material and will spit out the same answers. You should not only give the right answer but explain why and use an example. A personal experience, if possible."

Gerald pushed himself back from the table, dragging the chair across the linoleum as he did, knowing the scraping sound would piss off Emily. "It's not a good day when your girlfriend tells you you look and sound like a fool, and there's video proof of it."

Emily stood and stepped over Leo, who was sitting on the floor, eyeing his people equally in hopes of getting an impromptu ear scratch. She leaned in and softly whispered in Gerald's ear, "I never said you were a fool, just that you have to up your game with better delivery and more depth to your answers. Accomplish that, and you will crush the competition."

Gerald looked down at Leo and wished he could switch places with the cat. Leo had no worries about promotional boards, overtime, money, or making a fool of himself. Fucking cat.

Gerald, still defensive, said, "You know what I wish I could say." Emily straightened and crossed her arms. "I wish I could tell the promotion board that the PD is sliding into a malaise, stuck in its own plodding inertia, and that I could change that course."

"I'm pretty sure you don't want to denigrate your own workplace in front of a promotional board."

"Yeah, I know that. The place is frustrating sometimes. It's like the 'broken windows theory.' You know what that is, right?"

"The theory that small, unattended problems will affect people's attitudes and lead to larger problems."

"Right. Or put another way, if no one cares about the small problems, then they won't care about the big ones. In the PD, there are lots of small problems that no one cares about."

"Like what?"

"Cops that dodge calls consistently and junior guys

who help cover for them. Like some of the veterans never responding to a call so your junior backup takes it, writes the report, makes the arrest, everything. The street sergeants never know the difference because they don't pay attention to the radio. The guys getting sandbagged with the calls don't say anything because they don't want to be a rat, and the guys blowing off calls are sitting fat and happy. Small problem, right? At least the crime is being investigated."

"That still sounds pretty messed up."

"It is, and it leads to more shit. If it's okay to blow off your calls, then what else gets blown off? Some guys don't even roll as a backup when they are assigned to. I know of one recent incident where one of the newer guys never checked an alarm he was sent to, just filled out the form stating the business was secure. Turns out, the place was burglarized. The new kid gets called on the carpet and says his FTO had done the same thing during training, so he thought it was acceptable to do it."

"So you are saying it's becoming acceptable not to perform even the most basic functions of being a cop?"

"Right. And most of the bosses don't care or at least don't want to know."

"If you were a sergeant, do you think you could change that? Be the boss who cares and make sure things get done right?"

"I'd like to try."

"You're almost there. A little more dedicated practice, and you will come out number one. Then you can change the place from the broken windows PD to the exceptional PD or at least an exceptional squad."

Gerald took a deep breath and stared at the stack of study cards on the table. He had devoted most of his study time preparing for the written exam, now three days away, not worrying too much about the oral board. At present, he realized that he'd have to work just as hard, if not harder, for this second portion of the test.

"Thanks for listening to my bullshit. I'm going to set up in front of the bedroom mirror and practice how I can vocalize, enunciate, and deliver my answers like Lincoln delivering the fucking Gettysburg Address. Then maybe we can have sex."

Emily smiled, "It's not bullshit. You care about your job, and the people you work with, and I don't mind listening to you 'cause I care about you."

Emily leaned in, nibbled on his ear, and whispered, "And maybe we can have sex after you finish your homework."

Gerald smiled as he gathered up the index cards. He could feel the bonds to Emily becoming stronger.

19

Tuesday
August 8
2113 hours

"CAN I GET A UNIT to back up Twenty-Two on a car stop on Larrabee Street? She's got a misuse on a vehicle," came the dispatcher's voice over the radio. No one answered. All of the nearby patrol cars were busy fielding calls. "I'll back Twenty-Two," replied Sergeant Reilly. A minute later, he was parked behind Unit Twenty-Two, walking up to the passenger side of her cruiser. Officer Donna Harris was in the driver seat writing up the traffic ticket with FTO Gerald Dennen dressed in plain clothes riding in the right seat. Reilly knocked on the passenger's side window. "What've you got?" he asked, looking at both Donna and Gerald, not sure which officer was handling the stop.

Donna didn't look up, keeping her eyes on the ticket she was filling out, and rattled off the violations in bullet-point fashion. "Vehicle's not registered, operator is a lady, and she admitted she took the plate off of her old car and placed it on this one, which she just bought. The kid's not in a child seat, and the vehicle isn't insured."

Reilly leaned down to catch Gerald's eye. Gerald said, "She's getting to the point in her training where I'm sorta invisible, just observing and making sure nothing goes

190

wrong, so ask her any questions you would ask anyone of us, Sarge."

Reilly nodded and asked Donna, "How recently did she buy the vehicle?"

Donna shuffled through the paperwork the operator had given her. "According to this bill of sale, she bought it on July twentieth."

"Hmm, today's August eighth. Plenty of time to do it right," mused Reilly.

Donna felt an internal pressure to justify writing the ticket. "I could understand if she just bought it yesterday and is trying to make ends meet, but this lady's got a serious attitude towards me, like it's my fault she got caught. So I called for a tow. I know I should red-sticker the vehicle and wait twenty-four hours, but she just stopped in the middle of the road, probably assuming I'd approach her from the driver's side and hoping I'd get hit by a passing car. As far as I'm concerned, she parked in a hazardous location, and it's getting towed."

"Fine with me," replied Reilly.

Reilly was curious about Donna's assessment of the operator's attitude. In his experience, new cops sometimes go all hard-ass in their attitude toward citizens; they haven't developed the discretion of when to be tough and when to be mellow. At times, the citizen's attitude toward an officer was just the reflection of their own toward them.

Reilly walked up to the passenger side of the stopped vehicle, leaned forward, and aimed his flashlight beam onto the front seat. The driver was a Hispanic woman in her early forties, talking quickly and excitedly in a rapid-fire fashion into her cell phone. Glancing at the stripes on Reilly's sleeve, she talked some more into her phone. Pausing her conversation, the woman lowered her passenger side window and said, "Lieutenant Cantu wants to talk to you," extending her cell phone in Reilly's direction.

"I don't want to talk to him right now," replied Reilly.

The woman repeated Reilly's answer over the phone with added emphasis. Seconds later, Reilly's phone vibrated. He answered it. It was Cantu.

"The woman you have stopped there has a small child that needs to get to a bathroom right away. You guys should probably let her go so she doesn't make a complaint."

Reilly went through a mock conversation with Cantu in his head. *You're right, Lieutenant, we should let her go because it's obvious that this woman, because she's Hispanic and knows you, overrides common sense and basic child safety and, again because she's Hispanic and knows you, can drive around in an uninsured and unregistered vehicle and, well, I guess because she's Hispanic and knows you, she should do whatever she wants under the threat of making a complaint against us.* After a couple of deep breaths, Reilly answered, "I'm looking at the child right now, and she's sitting calmly in the back seat, Lieutenant. I don't believe the woman is telling you the truth, and we are doing everything by the book, so if she makes a complaint, I'm not going to worry about it."

"Okay, I just want to avoid any complaints. Having citizens, especially minority citizens, angry at the cops doesn't help us."

It doesn't help anybody to have citizens, regardless if they are a minority, driving around without insurance or a child seat for their kids. What the fuck does this lady's mood have to do with any of that?

"No worries, boss." Reilly hung up and walked back to Donna's window.

"Make special notes about her attitude and any comments she makes, so if she makes a complaint, we can paint a clear picture of how she's behaving," Reilly advised Donna as the tow truck arrived. "You can bet she'll be bending Cantu's ear later. And I'll make some special notes myself, covering what I observed."

"Almost makes you not want to stop a vehicle," Donna said.

"That's what they want," replied Reilly, continuing his thoughts silently as he walked back to his cruiser. *The shitheads of society want the cops to leave them alone so they can be shitheads and conduct their nefarious business unfettered, so they make false complaints, call the watch commander, and record your conversations on their cell phones. Then, when they are the victim of a crime, they call the cops and want a full CSI team to investigate, but then they're reluctant to cooperate. 'I don't know' becomes their most-used line of conversation, because to openly help the police is against their culture, even when they're the victims. Advocates for the poor and minorities, like my dear Lieutenant Cantu, endorse a grievance culture for the very people they're trying to help. Ingrained with the belief that they are disadvantaged because they're poor or a minority, they accept living in a violent neighborhood among drug dealers, gangs, and thieves. Somehow the cops become the enemy. Cantu and his kind just make it harder on the cops and worse for the citizens.* Reilly got back in his cruiser and drove away. . . . *Retirement can't come soon enough.*

20

Friday
August 12
2029 hours

SERGEANT MITCH REILLY CAUGHT UP to the Ford Explorer, speeding westbound on Burnside Avenue in the light rain, as it approached the sharp S-turns. The red and blue from his emergency lights reflected off of the Explorer. *He's going too fast.* The Explorer's brake lights came on too late as it entered the left turn, sliding, yawing, skidding to the right over the low curb hard enough to pop the left wheels off the ground. Reilly had slowed before the turn and had expected to witness a crash, but luck—and Reilly couldn't tell if it was dumb luck or drunk luck—had spared the Explorer. It suffered no noticeable damage as it stabilized on the manicured lawn of a funeral home and careened its way back onto the road. The Explorer's pace slowed, and Mitch stayed on its tail, radio mic in his right hand.

The radio was busy. Several car stops were being performed, a motor vehicle accident was just called in, and a verbal domestic was reported. Mitch couldn't get a word in edgewise as he followed the Explorer, now doing less than twenty miles per hour, onto a side street lined with multifamily houses. The Explorer jerked left onto a driveway behind a three-family house with a half-dozen TV satellite dishes bolted to the exposed rear staircase.

Mitch clipped the mic back onto the radio, forgoing

calling off the stop or asking for backup. He parked his SUV cruiser inches from the rear bumper of the Explorer, aimed his spotlight into the rear-view mirror of his target, and approached the driver's side door. Right hand on his gun, his left hand held his flashlight up and away from his body. Sliding his hand from his weapon, he rapped on the window with his knuckle and got no response, so he tried again, a little harder. Nothing. Mitch flipped the latch on the door and flung it open, placing the flashlight beam straight into the eyes of the driver.

The man in the light beam was glassy-eyed, slack-jawed, and had a sixteen-ounce can of Modelo beer between his knees. His lips formed the definition of a stupid grin. His front-seat passenger was either feigning being asleep or actually was.

"What's going on tonight, guys?" Mitch asked.

The stupid grin became wider, but no words came from it.

"Talk to me, guys. Whose vehicle is this?"

"*No habla ingles.*"

"You don't speak English?"

"*No . . . No . . . No ingles.*"

There was no doubt in Mitch's mind the guy he was trying to talk to didn't speak English. Mitch estimated the operator was a worker, maybe a hard worker, probably recently arrived and not aware that in the USA, we don't get blitzed and drive around. Wherever he came from, that may be okay, but not here and not now.

"ID," Mitch said, miming with his forefinger and thumb to see his license or identification card. The operator just bobbed his head up and down. Mitch poked at the operator's ass; he could see that he had a wallet. The drunk leaned away from Mitch, allowing him to grab the wallet out of the pocket. Mitch placed his flashlight under his left armpit and fingered through the contents of the wallet. Some cash, an international driver's license, and a piece of scrap paper with phone numbers scribbled on it.

Mitch removed the international driver's license and held it up. "This no good. This fake. No such thing as an international driver's license." Stupidity just stared back.

Mitch knew what the rest of the process would be to arrest an apparent illegal, Spanish-speaking immigrant, as it had become a common occurrence. First, Reilly would need to find an officer who was fluent in Spanish to explain the curbside sobriety test, followed by the interpreter helping explain the Intoxilizer machine and booking process. Before locking him up for the night, Reilly would have to run the drunkard's fingerprints to see if he could find his true identity. Against the governor's wishes, Immigration and Customs Enforcement would be notified. In the morning, the drunk would be released regardless of whether his identity was confirmed. Undoubtedly, he would skip out on his court date.

Fuck that.

"This is what I'm going to do, you dumb motherfuckers." Mitch reached in and snatched the keys out of the ignition. "I'm going to throw all these keys into the sewer. You shitbag illegal fucks can figure it out from there."

Mitch walked to the middle of the road to a manhole cover and turned so the operator, now leaning out of his seat and cranking his head around to watch, could see what he was about to do. Dangling the keys for a moment, Mitch shook them, so they faintly chimed. He then dropped the keys to the steel cover. With his flashlight beam focused on the keys, he toed them with his spit-shined boot to the hole in the middle of the cover and slid them—car keys, house keys, all the keys on the ring—through the hole. The look of drunken stupidity became a look of drunken confusion, and belatedly a look of drunken concern. Even to the drunk, this was no longer funny.

Mitch climbed back into his cruiser. He kept the lights flashing as he drove away, inhibiting the drunk from observing his car number. He spit the words out as he drove: *Fucking no habla ingles illegal motherfuckers only a few more weeks of this shit Jesus fucking Christ I can't wait to get away from all these assholes!*

21

Tuesday
August 22
0930 hours

ARRIVING AT HEADQUARTERS AN HOUR before he had to be there, Gerald walked into the locker room with his dress uniform, class A's, slung over his shoulder. The uniform was wrapped in dry cleaner's cellophane, a shield against any last-minute dirt or dust. In a gym bag, he had his shoes, spit-shined and wrapped in a soft cloth to protect them. He would make a second trip to his vehicle, retrieving his leather gear, gun belt adorned with only a holster and handcuff case. *It will be over before you know it,* he told himself as he made the trips back and forth. The last step to pass, last chance to max out his promotion score, started in less than an hour.

Gerald had received his invitation to the oral board ten days earlier from the town Department of Human Resources in the mail. The brief note had congratulated him on passing the written portion of the test (though his test score did not appear in the note) and had instructed him to arrive at headquarters' second-floor meeting room at 10:30 on the twenty-second. The letter also advised him that the uniform of the day for all promotion candidates would be class A's.

Two weeks earlier, after completing the written test, Gerald had allowed himself a few days to relax. He felt confident he had performed well on the written test; he'd had to guess at just five of the hundred questions. His confidence grew after he joined other candidates for a beer after the test. "What did you put down for this question?" was the theme of the post-exam conversations. Gerald didn't offer what his responses were. Instead, he listened to the debates the others were having. Some really knew what they were talking about. Others were way off base.

The notice for the oral board put a small knot in Gerald's stomach. It also sent him into high gear. Daily he practiced answering questions from his index cards. He peppered lieutenants and sergeants for additional topics discussed in past boards. Those topics became more mock questions on his index cards, leading to longer practice sessions with Emily. Emily graded him each time, promising him a private strip show and sex, however he wanted it, if he achieved a perfect score. Emily delivered on her promise. Gerald never posted a perfect score, and she didn't provide her sex reward.

"Get those stripes, and I'll be your fantasy woman," was her new promise.

Now he checked himself in the full-length mirror in the locker room. His class A's were impeccable. Satisfied, he walked down the hall, ascended the stairs to the second floor, and passed through the security door leading to the second-floor lobby—a public access area squeezed between two secure wings of the building. *I'm calm, confident, ready to show them what I know.* Halfway across the lobby, he reached into his back pocket to retrieve his wallet. It wasn't there. No wallet, no key card to unlock the security entrance leading to the meeting room, where the board sat, only about ten paces from where he stood. The door behind had clicked shut. *Damn it! How can I be so stupid to leave my wallet in my locker?* Aiming for perfection had distracted him from his regular routine of grabbing his wallet before securing his locker. His watch showed 10:25. *Now would be a good time for one of the useless admin types, who walk around all day with a sheet of paper in their hands trying to look busy, to walk through one of these doors.* He waited and paced. His well-orchestrated timing was falling apart by the second. Using public access hallways and a staircase to the desk officer's location to pick up a key, then getting back up here, would take time. Maybe too much. Creating a loud disturbance, maybe pounding on the thick security door to attract attention, could possibly alert the board that some idiot, *Gerald*, was locked out. Not the way to make a first impression. Hoping for someone to come through, he checked his watch again: 10:27. He could feel sweat building under his uniform. *Shit!*

22

Friday
September 2
0003 hours
Chapter 1 continued

WHEN A BULLET RIPS THROUGH the brain, the body's central nervous system instantly shuts off. The body containing the destroyed brain falls where it stood, collapsing on top of itself, the upper body flopping to whichever side the downward momentum pushes it. With the life switch flipped off, the body falls into a heap.

The call Donna was fielding had come in over her radio, first the address then the nature of the call, "Take a suicide by handgun, sounds like it just happened." Less than a block away from the location of the suicide when the dispatch came in, Donna was going to be the first cop there, alone. She had no idea if she could handle what she was about to undergo. In her previous three months of training under an FTO, she had never experienced a call like this.

Her legs carried her unwilling mind forward in the dark, quiet night as she slow-jogged to the light coming through the front door and kitchen window. Rapping on the door with the butt of her flashlight, she called out, "Police, police officer!"

"We're back here."

Donna entered the house and stepped through the kitchen into the living room. There, her eyes became focused on the adult male, unconscious, legs and hips turned to his side, his back to the floor, shoulders flat, face up. Blood steadily flowed out of the side of his head, as if from a garden hose turned on halfway. Donna became dizzy, the numbness in her legs moved upward toward her chest, and grayness entered her peripheral vision. She sensed more than saw people sitting on a couch to her right, watching her. *I have to do something. I can tell they are looking at me. They are expecting me to do something. I don't know what to do.*

The pool of blood was getting bigger. *You have to do something. Might as well dive right in. Keep moving. Keep doing something!*

Donna reached down and grabbed the victim's wrist, feeling for a pulse. There was one, rapid and weak. *Still alive, holy shit! How much blood is in the human body 'cause it's still flowing out of him?* "Get medical up here ASAP," Donna said into her shoulder mic, forgetting to include her unit number, not that it mattered. EMS had been alerted at the same time Donna caught the call and was on its way. She knew that but wanted them here *now!*

She stood and looked at the three people sitting on the couch, one young woman between two young men, and stated the obvious. "There's not anything I can do. EMS is already on their way." Then she asked the obvious, "What happened?" The three pairs of eyes barely blinked, staring into Donna's eyes. She was the only thing to look at besides the mess on the floor, and they weren't going to look at that anymore.

The woman answered, "He's my cousin, lives next door with my aunt. He came in, mumbled something, then said, 'I'm sorry.'"

One of the men on the couch spoke softly, "He had a gun in his hand . . . put it to his head . . . heard a sound like a small firecracker. Then he was on the floor . . . didn't think it was real till we saw the blood."

"He shot himself. Where's the gun?" Donna asked.

The three broke their gaze and glanced around the room, barely moving their heads. "I dunno," the same male said in a subdued voice.

The grayness had vanished from edges of Donna's vision; her mind had clicked in and was engaged with her duties. She was still numb. Adrenaline was mixing with the fear. The victim was dying, can't help him. Triage the scene. She propped opened the front door and pushed the kitchen table and chairs into a corner, giving EMS a straight shot into the living room. *Where the fuck are they?* Going back into the living room, she again surveyed the dying man and the room. The blood flow from the wound had slowed, almost stopped. The blood puddle was as big as it would get, it looked like close to a gallon had spread onto the bare hardwood floor. The three on the couch weren't moving or even talking. Donna thought about moving the figure to look for the gun, guessing it had dropped to the floor before the body fell on top of it. She was running through how she could move an inert the body on her own without stepping into the puddle when three paramedics came up behind her, crowding into the small room.

"I'm guessing there a loaded gun under him, so be careful," she said to the first paramedic in line. Unshouldering his medical bag and kneeling down next to the victim, the EMT donned his medical gloves. The other two stood still, keeping their gear shouldered. They weren't going to unpack for this one. The first paramedic checked for vital signs and said, "He's still alive, but . . ."

Donna surveyed the scene. In her mind, she was floating above the group of people thrown together in this cramped living room. The three spectators on the couch, three paramedics, one of whom was actually playing a role, the one cop who felt like she should be directing but didn't know where to look for a cue, and the one newly deceased playing his role perfectly.

A tap on her shoulder led to instant relief when she

turned and saw Sergeant Reilly easing up next to her. "What have you got so far?" he asked.

"Apparently, he shot himself in the head in front of the three on the couch, at least one of whom is a relative. Paramedic says he's still alive, but they aren't doing anything."

Reilly leaned down and asked the paramedic kneeling on the floor, "You guys going to transport him?"

"No, we're not."

Reilly bent down closer to the one paramedic next to the body; he was the one who was doing the talking. "His family is right here. At least get him out of the house."

"Nope, we're not doing that."

Reilly was at a loss for words as the paramedic turned and consulted a portable ECG machine. The paramedic stated, "He's dead. We don't transport dead bodies. I'll put the time of presumption of death on our run sheet and leave it on your watch commander's desk." There was no further conversation with the paramedics as they quickly vanished.

Reilly summoned two patrol units to help Donna, directing them to interview the three witnesses separately, away from the scene, stressing the importance of swabbing the hands of each witness for gunshot residue (GSR). That task completed, he called for a crew from the medical examiner's office to respond and pick up the body for a postmortem examination. The shock of the scene barely registered with Reilly. Getting the steps of the investigation done completely and correctly occupied his mind.

Officers and witnesses removed, Reilly stood alone in the house and took in the scene one more time. If the suicide happened the way the witnesses stated, then there might be evidence of the round from the gun impacting a wall, piece of furniture, broken window, something. He stepped around the blood puddle and examined the rear wall. No damage to the blinds over the window, and the window was intact. Squatting, he found what he was looking for. Hiding in the shadow of the windowsill molding was a small hole in the sheetrock, roughly the same size as the entry wound to the victim's head. He knelt by the window and toyed with the idea of cutting out the sheetrock with his buck knife to find whatever was left of the fatal bullet when he sensed a presence behind him. He turned his head as saw a gentleman a few years older than he standing at the edge of the living room, his clenched fists jammed into baggy jeans, his placid face staring down at the dead body. *Fuck! I didn't put crime scene tape out, and this guy walked right in.*

"Who are you?" Reilly asked.

Softly the gentleman replied, "I'm his father."

Reilly stepped around the body and blood toward the father. The natural order of life had been reversed; parents aren't supposed to see their children die. Behind the emotionless face was a confused mind. "I'm sorry, sir. It's best if you weren't in here. Let's go stand on the front stoop and get some air. Whatever we can do for you tonight, we'll do." The father turned around as Reilly put his arm around his shoulder and gently guided him through the kitchen and out the front door.

Hours later, as the false dawn was beginning to glow to the northeast, the only sound was the soft rumble from Donna's cruiser engine. The peace belied the events and confusion of a few hours earlier. Reilly walked up to the driver's side of Donna's cruiser and, bending his head down, said, "The ME's officers have just left with the body. Evidentiary has retrieved the bullet from the wall, GSR'd the victim's hands, and completed their photo shoot." He leaned down a little closer and observed Donna's face for a few moments, trying to assess the reaction of the department's newest officer to the earlier scene.

Donna tapped away on the keyboard to her MDT then paused, and, expecting Reilly to ask how far along she was on her report, began stating her synopsis to him without being prompted. "Based on the three independent statements, and finding the gun under the victim, this truly does appear to be a suicide."

"What did the witnesses say?" Reilly asked. Donna pulled down the three handwritten statements she had filed in the visor over her head and flipped through them, picking out small passages from each. "He's a soldier . . . returned from a year in Afghanistan and found out his wife had found another guy to live with. He had been trying to get her to move back in with him, but supposedly, she had told him she doesn't love him anymore. . . . He loved her and had said several times in the recent past, past couple of weeks, he couldn't live without her. . . . He's been acting depressed compared to his old outgoing self . . . recently quit his job . . . owned a Colt M1911 .45, which appears to be the gun we recovered."

"How were the witnesses related to the victim?"

"The young lady and one of the guys are cousins. The second guy was a close friend to all of them. All three said it happened so fast they couldn't believe their eyes at first."

"Keep typing. I'm guessing the results from the GSR kits will back up the statements and show the witnesses will have clean hands, and the victim won't. Hopefully, that will put to rest any blame or conspiracy theories amongst family members."

Donna nodded faintly and said, "The conspiracy theories may be put to rest, but the ex-wife, whatever she is, will be getting a shit-ton of blame."

"I'm sure she will." Reilly stood and said, "The father is waiting for his ex-wife, the kid's mother, to wake up in the home next door before he tells her the news. He says she sleeps with earplugs and eye mask, so she apparently slept through the whole thing earlier. He wants me to be there when he tells her, and I said I would."

"Should I go in with you?"

"Naw. Just keep writing."

Reilly walked away, and Donna became absorbed in

writing her report, losing track of time, when she heard the scream. *Mom's awake and got the news.* Even from the street, Donna could feel the tormented anguish in the wailing, the only distinguishable word, "NO!" repeated often. Screams were still punctuating the diminishing volume of the mother's crying when Reilly exited the front door. When he passed by Donna's open window, it looked like he was trying to force a smile that wouldn't come. She heard him say, "Front row seat. . . . We're clear from here."

The final two hours passed, and the end of the shift came quickly for Donna. The rest of the officers from the midnight shift had already left by the time she had her report completed and signed off. As she changed into street clothes in the empty locker room, the images she saw earlier were still clear in her head, and she wondered when, or if, they would go away. She was tired but wide awake and knew sleep wouldn't come quickly today like it usually did after working through the overnight.

Walking to her personal vehicle, she saw Sergeant Reilly had parked his truck next to her car and was sitting on the open tailgate. He had a coffee in his hand, and music was coming from the speakers of his truck. "How do you feel?" he asked when she got closer.

"I'm not tired like I usually am after a midnight shift," she said.

"Was that your first time getting to a scene like that by yourself?"

"Yeah, I just got off FTO a little over a week ago. Most of my calls have been bullshit domestics, alarms, and minor car accidents, so this morning was my first bad call."

"From what I saw, you did good, real good. Those calls suck, but every one of us who has worked this job has had to handle them, and you handled it as well as any veteran."

"Thanks, Sarge." The praise, a sign of acceptance into the police fraternity, soothed Donna.

Reilly tapped his temple and asked, "How's things up here?"

"Okay, I guess. I don't know how I'm supposed to feel. . . . It was an adrenaline rush. I don't feel sad, but it was a sad thing to happen. What I saw is still fresh in my mind. I'm tired, but I'm not tired. Sorry, my thoughts are a little disjointed, I guess."

"All perfectly normal things to feel. Are you working tonight?"

"No. I have the next three days off."

Reilly pursed his lips and nodded then said, "It is usually better for someone who has gone through a scene like that to work the next day, be around others who have been through the same experience. Get back on the horse kinda thing."

"I'll be doing the opposite. Couple of girlfriends have rented a cottage down at Misquamicut Beach, and I was going to take a quick nap and drive down to join them."

"Any of them cops or first responders?"

"No. College friends. One is living in Rhode Island, and one is in Massachusetts. It will be kind of a mini-reunion."

"Enjoy your weekend. My career is at its end, but there's still a few more days I have to report in. When you get back, if you're comfortable talking to me, feel free to call any time, even after I retire."

"I appreciate that. I'll keep it in mind."

"Officially, as a supervisor, I am also reminding you that we have several officers who are employee assistance program counselors, EAP for short, if you feel the need to talk to them. As a fellow cop who's been exposed to the inner workings of this department, I would advise not talking to them, since there is no confidentiality between you and the EAP counselor." Donna cocked her head. "Trust me, most of them will up-channel everything you say to a chief within minutes of you saying it."

Donna took Reilly's advice and opinion with a grin. She hadn't yet arrived at the point where she felt the need to talk to someone about the suicide. At the same time, she couldn't fathom a fellow cop repeating something she would say in confidence. She changed the subject. "What's the music playing in your truck?"

"Cowboy Junkies. Very mellow. Helps me unwind on the way home."

Donna pulled her phone out from her back pocket and poked at it with her index finger several times. After a few more seconds of silence, she looked up from her phone and said, "Got it on my phone now. I'll listen to it on my way home."

"Have fun at the beach."

23

Friday
September 10
0024 hours

DONNA WAS DUTIFULLY PATROLLING HER beat, District
Thirty, which was comprised of Main Street and its
bars. She didn't need coffee to stay awake, merely
being by herself in the cruiser, depending on only herself
to know where she was or how to respond to any given call
or interview a suspect or handle any scene she had not yet
experienced kept her on alert. The suicide call a week earlier
had nearly overwhelmed her, but now, after going through
that ordeal, she had more confidence in herself to handle
almost anything. *It can't be worse than that,* she reasoned.

"District Thirty, check on a vehicle at Center and Main.
Got a call of smoke coming from a vehicle parked in the
middle of the intersection."

Donna responded with a "Ten-four," and, after rounding a
couple of street corners, came upon an older two-door silver
sedan parked in the travel lane facing the stoplight. Smoke
and steam emanated from the grill and edges of the hood.
Donna announced her arrival to dispatch over the radio,
stepped out of her cruiser, and approached the driver's side
door of the steaming vehicle.

There, seated in the driver's seat, was a white male, about
thirty years old, motionless, eyes closed, his chin firmly
resting on his chest, his belly mushed against the bottom

210

of the steering wheel. A pint of coffee brandy was wedged between his thighs. Donna opened the door, reached in, and turned off the ignition. She noticed the driver had one foot on the accelerator and one on the brake.

"Hey, wake up," Donna said. "Time to wake up, sir." No response. Donna shook the driver's shoulder and yelled a little louder, leaning in toward his left ear.

His eyes slowly opened as he sluggishly turned his head to face Donna. "Fuck you," he slurred.

Donna watched for a moment as the driver fumbled for the gearshift, his right foot mashing the gas pedal. "Come on, step out of the car," Donna said again.

"Fuck you, asshole."

Donna grabbed the driver's shirtsleeve and began to tug, trying to remove him from the vehicle before he figured out that he was one twist of the ignition key away from driving. The fat man's reaction to Donna's attempt to remove him was slow, but before Donna could get him out of the driver's seat, the thick fingers of his right hand clutched the steering wheel. The left hand was groping for the door. Donna was losing her grip on his shirtsleeve and could see she might lose this confrontation. *Where the head goes is where the rest of the body goes* was the mantra of the defensive tactics instructors in the academy and at the PD.

Donna let go of the sleeve and grabbed the driver's thick hair with both hands, yanking his head hard to the side and back. His grip on the wheel loosened. Donna placed him in a headlock and twisted her body to the left. Her leverage popped the fat bastard out of the vehicle and onto the pavement. His sluggish mind, too slow to keep up, couldn't order his legs to get under him and stand up. Donna was quick to bounce back onto her feet; her left hand fingered the snap to her pepper spray and slid the small canister into her palm. A second pair of hands suddenly appeared, and the fat man's right arm was deftly whipped, twisted, and folded behind his back. Donna grabbed the second flabby arm and repeated the arm-twisting move, ending it with her cuffs clicking around the drunk operator's thick wrists.

Sergeant Gerald Dennen stood back and looked at Donna. "This is where you tell me why you're body-slamming a drunk."

"I didn't think I had much of a choice," Donna started as she told Gerald what had happened in the previous thirty-five seconds, including her very real fear the driver would push her away and drive off in a highly intoxicated state.

"Good work," Gerald said with a slight smile. "Make sure you write it up just the way you told me. Let's get this asshole into your cage."

The two officers leaned against Gerald's cruiser, catching their breath after heaving the heavy drunk off the pavement and squeezing him into the rear seat cage of Donna's cruiser. Gerald said, "I heard you had to handle a fresh suicide a few days ago."

"Yeah, it was a mess."

"Those are hard. Especially when you are the first one there and by yourself."

"Yeah," Donna paused, then asked Gerald, "How do you handle the days after those calls?"

"I give myself three days. If, after three days, I can't shake the sights or emotions of something like that, then I have to have a real honest conversation with myself. A self-check to see if I can handle this job."

"You're still here, so I'm guessing you've self-checked yourself to stay on the job."

"I have conversations with other people, but I like to think I can make the decision myself." Donna remained quiet. Gerald felt he had to say more. "Self-check or internal coaching, whatever you want to call it, it's worked for me so far. But for it to work, you have to be honest with yourself. I guess what I'm saying is you will experience more calls like that, and if you can't handle them, if they start to dominate your thoughts and influence your life, then maybe this line of work isn't for you."

"It's a little late to be advising me of that now, isn't it?"

"Gotta go through the experience first."

Donna inhaled deeply and smiled, "It wasn't a 'good times' call, but it was definitely a front row seat." She turned and looked a Gerald, "Thanks, Sarge. At the moment, I feel pretty good. And by the way, those stripes look good on you."

"If it wasn't for Lynn in dispatch, I wouldn't have got them."

"Why's that?"

"With only two minutes to spare before my oral board, I was stuck on the second-floor lobby outside the security door without my key card. Lynn happened to see me in the surveillance camera over the door. She walked upstairs and let me in. I made it with thirty seconds to spare."

"Sounds like you owe Lynn."

"I did, so I bought her and all the dispatchers on day shift a dozen donuts and box of coffee."

"That was nice of you." Donna turned to look at the drunk in the back of her cruiser and said, "I guess I should get going on processing this guy."

"You do that, and I'll wait for the wrecker. Then I'll buy you a cup of coffee."

24

Tuesday
September 19
1148 hours

REILLY BAITED HIS HOOK AND sent it down into the dark water of Long Island Sound. His center console powerboat, christened *Slow Worker,* dipped to whichever side he was standing. At twenty-two feet, it wasn't the biggest fishing boat on the Sound, but it was one of the more successful ones. He already had two stripers on ice, each about thirty-five pounds; one more and he would head back to his marina in Niantic and display his catch, his latest trophies, on the dock, laying the fish side by side while he scrubbed *Slow Worker* clean. His exhibit of pelagic prowess would catch some compliments and more than a few looks of envy from the other fishermen in the marina.

The previous two weeks had been busy. He had put in his retirement papers on a Friday afternoon, handing the chief's secretary an official memo giving the department the customary two week's notice. The secretary, ever efficient, made three copies—one for Reilly's personnel file, one for the chief, and one for Reilly. The chief was busy at the moment, the secretary had told Reilly, but she could schedule an appointment for him to meet with the chief if he wanted. "That's okay," Reilly told her, thinking to himself that it was up to the chief to invite you to an exit interview, not the other way around.

Reilly had barely made it back to the sergeant's office, one floor below and on the opposite side of the building, when the chief stepped in. He was smiling and could be described as almost chipper.

"You've put in your two weeks' notice. I didn't know you were thinking about retiring."

Reilly shrugged his shoulders, "You know how it is around here, Chief. It's best to keep one's personal plans to oneself. Keeps rumors from starting."

"Yes, right. If you need anything, anything at all, don't be afraid to call. I'd be happy to help you."

"Thanks, Chief. I'll keep that in mind."

"Do you have any plans? I'd be happy to write a recommendation for you if you are looking for another job."

"No real plans right now, Chief. I have my eyes on a nice little fishing boat. I think I'll do a little fishing through the end of the summer, then figure out my next move."

Reilly's response was only a partial truth. The chief didn't deserve any sincerity from Reilly. *Slow Worker* had already been purchased; she was a pre-owned boat with only two seasons of use on her. The old sergeant had also decided to remain gainfully unemployed. If he did return to the workforce, it would be helping out at the marina where *Slow Worker* was docked, or maybe at his local liquor store recommending wines or single-malt Scotches to naive customers. Chiefs looked at officers like Reilly as low achievers, folks who have limited abilities and foresight, or are just lazy. They ask: Who retires at a fairly early age with no five-year plan? Reilly and his ilk looked at the demographic of police chiefs as political players with limited investigative skills and personal rectitude. There were exceptions, of course. There was the Hartford deputy chief who arrived at the Hartford Hospital intensive care unit a few years earlier when one of Reilly's officers was critically injured. He met the injured officer's family and friends, offered condolences and kind words of encouragement, and assigned a patrolman to be on the ICU floor 24/7 to assist the family in any way. The HDC had a reputation of getting out of his cruiser and chasing down suspects. He wore a policeman's uniform every day; he didn't look at street work as dirty. In contrast, Reilly's chief's visit to the ICU was perfunctory and uncomfortable. The North Hayward chiefs preferred to wear suits and jackets. Uniforms appeared to be beneath them, as was the dirty street work. Their five-year plans were to be a police chicf somewhere else. To Reilly's knowledge, no North Hayward chief ever was a successful chief anywhere else. They either got fired or quit within weeks of commanding a dissimilar police department.

"Again, Mitch, anything you need, let me know."

"Will do, Chief." The chief was quickly gone, a pep in his step and grin, or maybe a smirk, on his face. *Motherfucker is happy to see me go. Cunt.*

The next two weeks were normal for Reilly as far as police patrol functions went. Some patrol cops get paranoid at the end of their professional tour and don't want to venture out onto the street. They feel a car wreck during a chase or wrestling with an armed suspect will permanently alter their retirement plans. Reilly just went through the motions right up to the moment of his last signoff with dispatch. He knew what was coming and had to control his voice as he keyed the mic. "Unit Forty, take me off-line." Dispatch replied, "Unit Forty, roger, stand by." Then each dispatcher came on the air and said goodbye. His squadmates came on air next, one at a time, each with kind words, and Reilly replied to each, working hard to keep his delivery even. The last signoff, last words over the police radio, the last time he would sit in a cruiser. It was over. Reilly sat for a few moments, wrapping himself in the moment, unsure of what he was feeling. Relief, yeah. Sense of accomplishment, maybe. Sad, a little bit. Tired, yup.

Reilly's semi-official farewell, otherwise known as the "Cake and Shake," was scheduled on a Friday morning, a scheduled day off for Reilly but his actual last day of employment. The official farewell ceremony would be the following spring and would include all officers who had retired in the previous twelve months. The Cake and Shake gathering is the immediate social function to showcase the department's gratitude to a retiree. It can be a dicey affair. A large cake is purchased, and notices are placed on bulletin boards around headquarters, and emails are sent out: "*So and so*" *is retiring. Come and say goodbye to "so and so" at 10:00, Friday. Cake and refreshments will be served.* Sometimes no one shows up. A chief and some admin personnel will always be there, but there's no guarantee one's current or former squadmates, past investigative partners, supervisors, or subordinates will be in attendance. The empty chairs speak volumes in those cases. *"So and So" who?* Some retiring officers skip the Cake and Shake altogether, out of the fear of walking into a barren room.

Reilly had thought of skipping the affair, but an old retired friend told him that it would be the only time the good people that supported his work—records clerks, dispatchers, and secretaries—would get to see him and say goodbye. Some of them had known him for years, but the professional interactions were limited mostly due to his odd shifts, with him working when most of them weren't. Reilly thought about it and agreed with that observation. It could come off as arrogant to leave without saying goodbye.

Reilly had attended enough Cake and Shakes to know how the event would unfold. The retiree is invited to the front of the training room, and one of the chiefs reads a prepared statement citing the positions and highlights of his or her career. A plaque trades hands. There are some gratuitous words from the chief and an opportunity for the retiree to say something. Reilly wanted to say thank you in a nice way but also let the chief know what he thought of him.

Friday morning, stepping off the elevator across from the training room, Reilly felt the same anxiety he used to feel before going on a raid. *I hope there's more than a couple folks in there.*

Reilly shook the chief's hand, turned to address the full room, and said, "When I started this job, I had no real idea what I would see or do. I imagined being the tough good guy cop you see in movies and TV shows, the go-to guy who knows all the answers, and when necessary, can go it alone. I imagined an uncompromising brotherhood that's forged from shared experiences that few outside of police work know. Boy was I ignorant.

"As it turned out, this is what I would see and do. I would hold an infant, a victim of Sudden Infant Death Syndrome, and listen to detectives delicately ask the family questions no one wants to ask. I would attend postmortem exams and always be amazed at how the human body is put together and how fragile it is. Early in my career, images of broken bodies were hard to wash away from my mind. After a few years, my mind would be clean of any bad images before the end of the shift. Early in my career, I would stand in the middle of a homicide scene and have no idea what to do next. Later in my career, I would stand in a homicide scene and know exactly what I wanted done and how.

"I've seen the town at one hundred miles an hour with the tired cruiser's siren and lights wailing and flashing. Fun stuff.

"I've seen a fleeing drug dealer, murder suspect, car thief, and asshole criminal try to outrun a K9 German shepherd. That never got old. The dog always won, and I have to admit, I enjoyed watching those arrestees' pain as the dog's fangs dug into their flesh.

"I've enjoyed the sense of righteousness when arresting a violent domestic partner. Catching a car thief in the act. Chasing down a burglar in the night woods. I've tracked footprints in the fresh snow over fences and highway lanes, jogging and running for the better part of an hour to catch a home invasion suspect who had kicked in the door of his ex-girlfriend's house. That gave me job satisfaction.

"I've seen the look in drug dealers' eyes as we kicked in their doors or ripped them out of their cars. Total surprise. They never saw it coming. In the narcotics unit, we performed undercover drug deals every day and drug raids every week. Yes, kicking in a door and screwing your Glock into the side of some dealer's head and saying, 'Caught ya!' is a blast. Performing undercover buys, I was scared every time. But my fear was my problem, not anyone else's. You do the buy and move on.

"I've seen and been a part of the high-risk entry dance while a member of the Emergency Response Team. That was teamwork at its best.

"What else have I seen. . . . I've seen high-ranking individuals spread unsubstantiated rumors of officers in this department. Often re-energizing the rumor with urgent updates to certain members of the department knowing full well, the whispers will spread. I've known of co-workers who would not want to come to work, not because of the risk or the environment on the street, but because of the stench of the environment inside this building.

"I've seen the success of the administration's strategy to keep the union weak by creating infighting amongst the members. A divided union is easier for the administration to handle. The strategy has also killed department camaraderie.

"I've seen rookie cops make instant life-or-death decisions while their supervisors failed to respond to the scene—their bosses either purposely unaware, uncaring, or simply just cowards.

"Today is the last day I will be seen as a member of this police department. It's been quite a ride, and I have no regrets."

Reilly didn't say any of that.

Reilly turned and shook the chief's hand and said thanks.

He turned and faced the room full of officers, records division staff, and dispatchers. He mumbled something about missing them already, and good luck, and be safe. More words wanted to come out, but Reilly couldn't get them in order. *Thanks for coming to say goodbye and let's have some cake.*

Bam! The rod nearly escaped his grip as a keeper tugged and pulled on the bait. *Oh yeah, you're a big one—come on, baby!* Reilly's hands and arms sequentially spun line onto the reel and pulled on the fishing rod. *Slow Worker* rocked as Reilly stepped back and forth from one end of the transom to the other, working his prize closer to the boat. Splash. Rod into holder. Net ready . . . lean over and scoop. *Ohh, you're a big one!*

The third striper was the biggest of the day and maybe Reilly's biggest catch ever. Reilly congratulated himself out loud—*You're a fishing machine. Fish fear you, man*—while placing the fish on ice in the large cooler strapped to the deck of *Slow Worker.*

On the way to his home port at full throttle, Reilly pumped his fist in the air, letting out a yelp as his boat pounded over the wake of the New London ferry.

After securing and scrubbing his boat, Reilly gathered his catch and ambled down the dock to the cleaning table. Working his knife around the bones of the stripers, carefully pulling off the meat, feeding scraps to the seagulls, and stuffing the fresh fillets into plastic bags, his mind drifted. He couldn't remember the last time he felt this good. Was it contentment? Whatever it was, he hadn't felt it for a long time, certainly not from the job of police work. Today his mind and hands had yielded food from the sea. Effort was rewarded. The efforts of twenty-five years of trying to do things right at North Hayward Police Department had brought some rewards but a lot of heartache too, and frustration. Maybe in time, he would feel the rewards of his job as a cop, but right now, Reilly was on top of the world being a fisherman.

Later, on the front porch of his home, Reilly sat with a cold beer and watched as his neighbors returned from a day's work. He waved each over to join him. One did, the others, shuttling between kids' soccer and lacrosse games, waved and smiled as they drove by.

After the sun had set, turning the evening colors gray, Reilly's neighbor, sufficiently intoxicated, walked back to his home across the street, only stumbling once. Alone, Reilly sat for a few minutes, holding a half-empty beer. His wife, still the love of his life and best friend, would be home soon, and he'd have dinner ready, but for now, it was quiet. Reilly took a deep breath through his nostrils and held it in. Slowly letting his breath out, he embraced the moment, cold beer, loving wife, good friends and neighbors, fishing all day. Who the fuck needs a five-year plan?

END

Acknowledgements

Writing is a lonely affair. Like distance running or cycling, you are on your own to provide the energy and endurance to finish the task. Just as the endurance athlete depends on a support crew of trainers, coaches and family, a new writer depends on editors, trusted friends and family to help get the final story to print. To that end I have numerous people to thank.

To make things simple I will go in chronological order. First to read the original story was Michael Santacroce. Mike is an author himself as well as a retired Marine Corps colonel and fighter pilot. We knew each other as kids in the same neighborhood and in recent years we get together once in a while to tell stories and drink a few beers. Mike was the first to read a rough draft and give me feedback with words of encouragement which meant a lot to me and kept me going when I felt like dropping the whole project. Next are editors Stacey Longo and Rob Smales. They are professionals who let me know I have a story here but I also have a lot of work to do. From there I rewrote and sent a copy off to my very good friends and former co-workers Curt and Eileen Stolt. Eileen gave me some insight into being a woman in law enforcement that I hope I translated into this book in a positive way. Curt gave me advice that was an epiphany: break the story down into two books, it would be cleaner and easier to follow. From Curt and Eileen's wise counsel the final version of Front Row Seat came into view.

Because this is a story on law enforcement, I wanted

the final edit to be performed by an editor with exposure to police work, someone who speaks the same language. I found that person in Julie Sprengelmeyer Serkosky. Julie is married to another very good friend and former co-worker/ retired cop Phil Serkosky. Besides being married to a police officer, Julie's experience with local news reporting in East Hartford, where I worked, also gave her an exceptional vantagepoint from which to review Front Row Seat. Julie's edits, comments and suggestions tied the whole story together. I am truly grateful for her work.

Finally, I have to give so much thanks to my wife, Kim. Besides being my wife, best friend, confidant and more, she has been a part of every step of the writing process. Without her this story would be nothing more than notes in my desk drawer. Love you babe, and thank you.

About the Author

Mark Andrew Kelly dropped out of college and enlisted in the United States Marine Corps, finding himself standing on the yellow footprints of Parris Island the day after his twenty-first birthday.

After six years, several awards, and numerous deployments around the world, Mark was honorably discharged from the Marines with the rank of sergeant.

In January 1991, he was hired by the East Hartford Police Department. In the following twenty-one years, he worked as a patrol officer, investigator in the detective bureau/vice and narcotics, sergeant in the detective bureau, sergeant in the patrol division, and operator on the Emergency Response Team. He received fifteen awards and commendations for exceptional service.

Since his retirement, Mark and his wife, Kim, have sailed their boat from the coast of Maine to Guadeloupe and back to their home in Connecticut. Now boatless, they split their time between Connecticut and Jackman, Maine. An aviation enthusiast his whole life, Mark has earned several ratings and flies as much as his budget allows.